FROM THIS
DAY
FORWARD

BY
SHANNON MYERS

Cover Design by: The Final Wrap

Formatting: Daryl Banner

First Printing: 2016

ISBN 978-0-9975348-0-1

DEDICATION

To my Husby. You have always pushed me to follow my dreams and without you, I never would've had the courage to do this. I'm so blessed to share this life with you. I love you more!

TABLE OF CONTENTS

PROLOGUE

I don't remember a day in my life when I wasn't wishing that I could go back to some point in the past and change the way things had happened. I was convinced that if I could just change a few of the details, then everything would be perfect. It was a lot like those "Create Your Own Adventure" stories that you would read as a kid. You picked one of several choices and it would direct you to a certain page based on what you chose. I could never choose just one scenario.

Don't get me wrong, I liked my life…I just felt as though something was always missing. I'm a bit of what you might call a perfectionist, and according to my therapist, a bit of a control freak (she uses a much more "medical sounding" term)—but, I'm getting ahead of myself. Perhaps I should start at the beginning.

PART ONE: BETRAYAL

CHAPTER ONE

"This is completely normal. It happens to a lot of women," I take deep breaths as I hold the cell phone in my hands. Oh—who am I kidding? This is the furthest thing from normal.

"Please tell me she's asleep- I need you."

My husband, Landon, had left his cell phone unlocked on the couch next to me. I'm not the type to pry, but his phone was buzzing incessantly with text alerts. I was only trying to silence it so I could go back to my *Glee* marathon on Netflix.

My mouth suddenly dry (and hands shaking), I log into his phone and begin scrolling through the countless messages and pictures. I feel bile rising in the back of my throat at the explicitness in front of me.

I hear the shower shut off and guiltily shove the phone down in between the couch cushions. I try to force myself to focus on the television screen, but my mind is wrapped up in what I just witnessed on my husband's cell phone. Landon walks in wearing nothing but sweatpants, slung low on his hips. He runs his hand through his damp hair and grins at me just as his phone signals another incoming text.

He looks around, almost frantically, for it. I pull it from between the couch cushions and stand up, using the side of the couch to steady myself- it's as if the entire room has tilted out from under me.

"Elizabeth—" He reaches his hand out, trying to snatch the phone out of my hand.

"It's too late, Landon." My voice sounds resigned.

He makes a move as if to embrace me.

"Don't you dare touch me!" I try to compose myself before continuing, "You're sleeping with her." I'd meant it as a question, but it comes out as a statement.

He makes a pained expression and I bring my hands up over my face at his confirmation, "Oh my God. You're sleeping with her! You are—it's all over your face!"

Landon holds his hands up, "Elizabeth, please calm down."

He begins going through all the stages: denial— "The texts were meant for someone else," anger—"Why were you going through my phone?" and finally acceptance— "I think I'm in love with her."

It's a common theme in marriages these days, right? I'm not some exception, I know that. However, because I never do anything small, the woman in question is none other than Katie-Landon's best friend's wife.

I mentally check out as he attempts to make the situation better by telling me that it's been going on for years. Four years to be exact. As in—the bastard met, dated, and married me all while screwing her. She was a bridesmaid in my wedding for crying out loud! Katie was so close to Landon and my circle of friends was quite small—some might say almost non-existent—the point is, I thought having her in my wedding would make us closer.

I'd spent my entire relationship with Landon trying to make Katie like me and wracking my brain after every get-together for what I had done wrong. It seemed my every attempt to win her over was met with coldness or some sarcastic remark. When Landon wasn't close by she'd even go so far as to comment on what I was eating- "It must be nice to just not care anymore." This was said at a birthday party where I'd chosen to have a second slice of pizza. How sick is that?

He tried to make us friends. She's everything I'm not- tall (I'm 5'4), brunette (I'm blonde), stick-thin (I like to eat! So sue me, because size 8 is not fat.) You know, she even had a few modeling gigs in college because of course she did. Yes, this is definitely not a normal situation.

A strange gasping, choking sound startles me back to reality only for me to realize I'm the one making it. I push past him (and his excuses) and run out onto the front porch. The sobs overtake me before I even make it two steps.

"Elizabeth, wait!"

I can hear him coming after me and I take off running down the block barefoot. I don't want to hear anymore. I can't bear it.

A few minutes later I stop and rest against a tree, taking deep breaths in an attempt to calm down. I don't know how much time passes before the chill in the air reaches me.

By the time I make it back to the house he's gone, just like that. There's a note scribbled on a napkin lying on the island, "*I'm sorry*." As if that alone could atone for our sham of a relationship. I rip it up, scattering the pieces across the kitchen.

It's at this point that I sort of fall apart, turn on my favorite radio station, and begin scrubbing the house from top to bottom— as if doing so will somehow fix my marriage in the process. As Christina Perri sings to her ex-lover and his jar of hearts, I sit on the kitchen floor with my scrubber in hand, letting more tears fall. I feel so stupid. How could I have not seen the signs right in front of me? When I complained that his friends didn't like me, Landon would just

15

say that I wasn't trying hard enough and that I came across as standoffish.

It isn't like there isn't some truth in that. I get into big crowds and I sometimes feel like a fish out of water. I get hot and feel as though I can't breathe—and then come the tears. It's like my body goes into fight or flight at the thought of being in close proximity to large groups of people. Really, I'm much more comfortable as a wallflower with a drink in my hand, observing those around me.

While not exactly understanding of my feelings, Landon never gave me any reason to distrust him. He wasn't coming home late at night, smelling of another woman's perfume with lipstick on his collar—*does it ever happen like that?* He was home at five forty-five every evening. On the weekends, he would go golfing with Mike (Yes, as in Katie's unwitting husband) and then we would usually head out to meet friends for dinner or catch a movie. I'm not saying it was the stuff of romance novels, but had someone told me he was having an affair a week ago, I would've sworn they were mistaken. I just don't know when he would've had the time and in a small west Texas town, it's hard to keep a secret.

I was born in Fort Worth and lived there until I was eight. My dad was a partner for an insurance firm and his company offered him a position as Managing Partner of their Lubbock branch.

We left behind friends and family to live in a city where we knew no one. I started a new school and suffered my first anxiety attack. The majority of the kids I went to school with had been together since kindergarten and they didn't take kindly to outsiders from the big city. Where I had been outgoing, I became painfully shy and somewhat of a loner.

16

My parents begrudgingly put me in therapy and I really think they thought I would be instantly cured.

Landon grew up in the area, but we didn't actually meet until we ended up working a local health fair in 2009. He was recruiting nurses to travel to exotic locations such as Boise, Idaho and Wilmington, Delaware where they would work short-term contracts until someone permanent could be found. I, on the other hand, was handing out toothbrushes and trying to find a dental assistant for the pediatric dental office I worked for- the second one was proving to be much more difficult than it sounded. Working with kids is a lot of fun, but it's definitely not for everyone. We wanted our patients to enjoy coming to our office and based on the people I'd met so far, the poor kids would be having nightmares for years.

I couldn't go back to my office without any leads on a candidate though. The office manager, Lauren, didn't accept failure. I'd worked side by side with her for six years at that point and I was still not entirely convinced she wouldn't fire me given the chance. She'd jokingly refer to me as her other half, but then she'd turn around in the next moment and make sure to point out every mistake I'd made. No, I had to find someone she could interview or else I'd hear about it for the next few weeks—so much pressure.

As fate would have it, mine and Landon's booths just happened to be right next to each other. When he walked in to set up, every eye was on him. At 6'4, he commanded the room. Even with a suit on, his body looked to be carved from stone. His tousled light brown hair and bright green eyes probably had every woman within a five-mile radius swooning. I'd never been a fan of beards, but the man pulled it off so well. Even though he could've had any woman there,

17

he chose me. He was constantly engaging me in conversation throughout the day, so much so, that I found myself meandering over to his booth just to be near him. He was so charismatic.

I did end up finding the perfect person for the job opening we had—even with the beautiful distraction in the booth next to me. Dara has been with our office ever since. The patients adore her fun, child-like nature and the parents like how detailed she is when discussing treatment plans and post-operative instructions. Hiring her not only got Lauren off my back, but earned me a lot of respect in the process.

When the day ended and we were tearing everything down, Landon offered to take our chairs back and as I went to hand him one, his fingertips brushed my arm, giving me instant chills. I blushed and looked up at him. He was grinning from ear to ear, and I noticed that he had a dimple in his left cheek as he said, "You felt that too. Good." He got my number and he didn't even wait twenty-four hours before he called.

The first few conversations we were on the phone until dawn. I remember needing to plug my cell phone in and sit against the wall while the battery charged. I cannot even recall the specifics of what we talked about, but I found myself falling fast for him. We married a year later and up until a few hours ago, I was content with my life.

I snap out of my reverie to find my floors gleaming and the clock on the stove informing me that it's now Monday morning and I've spent the hours I should've been sleeping lost to my memories.

CHAPTER TWO

I decide to call in sick as I am going to be of absolutely no use to anyone, waiting until seven fifteen when I know Lauren will be there. She's immediately on alert, "What's wrong? You never call in sick. What's going on?"

I bite my lip and try to get my voice under control, "Nothing's going on Lauren—I just have that stomach stuff that's been going around. Trust me; you want me to stay home."

"Okay," she says unconvincingly, "You just don't sound like yourself. Get some rest and we'll see you tomorrow."

I hang up the phone and wander aimlessly around the house, picking up stray drinking glasses, straightening pillows, arranging magazines—it's like I'm on autopilot.

I eventually make my way into the master bedroom where I stand for at least ten minutes, in silence, just staring at our king-sized bed. I can hear the whir of the ceiling fan blades, birds chirping outside—even a dog barking down the alley. There are all these reminders that life is still going on outside of this room, but in here it feels like a tomb. He's left me and I can't even muster the strength to cry at the moment—I wonder if that's a bad sign.

I come to find myself, staring into the bathroom mirror hanging over the vanity. I expect to look different—like someone who's just lost everything—but, minus the red-rimmed bloodshot eyes, it's still me staring back.

I check my phone to make sure I haven't missed any calls or texts before walking in to Landon's closet. I close my eyes and breathe deeply. It smells like him in here—like cedar wood shave soap and leather.

As I reach up to take one of his dress shirts off the hanger, I notice his handguns resting on the top shelf of the closet. He's got quite the collection. The darkest parts of my brain emerge. It would be so easy to take one and put myself out of this misery—this hell that I am now walking around in. I shake my head as if to clear these thoughts. No. What if my parents found me? I was all they had and I couldn't bear the thought of anyone finding me like that.

That alone is enough to jar me and I turn off the closet light, shutting the door behind me. I take his shirt and pull it on over my tank top, taking care to button every button, before burying myself under a mound of blankets in bed. I use his pillow just because I need to be enveloped in the smell of him. I close my eyes and let the darkness take over.

When I open them again, it's late afternoon. It takes me a minute to get my bearings and then a wave of grief crashes over me as a high speed film replays the last twenty-four hours in my head. I grab my phone off of the nightstand and check—nothing. I force myself out of bed and make my way over to the wine cabinet. Three forty-five in the afternoon? —Yeah, that's a perfectly acceptable time of day to have a drink. I hate wine (Landon's the wine drinker), but I hate feeling like this and it's all we have in the house. I just need to numb myself for a bit. I find a bottle of Shiraz and don't even bother with a glass. I tip the bottle back and shudder with the first taste. How can people drink this stuff?

Half a bottle later and I'm sitting on the hardwood floor in the living room, texting my best friend (and hairdresser), Jess. She's really the only confidante I have at the moment—I don't trust any of our "couple friends" as they were friends with Landon first. That and I've never gotten the impression that they thought I was a good match for their Landon.

"Jess— I need to talk. Something bad has happened."

Her response is immediate, **"Lizzie, what's going on?"**

She refuses to call me Elizabeth (like everyone else does)—because and I quote, *"It's an old woman's name."*

"Landon's gone."

"Oh my God—where are you? Are you okay? Of course you're not okay."

"No, I'm not okay. I'm at home—drinking."

"If you're drinking this early, it must be bad. Hold tight and I'll be over as soon as I can."
"Bring me some champagne. We've only got wine here."

"Will do, just give me a bit to finish up with my last client and I'm all yours."

I'm just about to pick myself and my almost empty wine bottle up off the floor when my phone buzzes with an incoming text. It's Jess again.

"Lizzie, I love you. Just try to relax and I'll be there soon."

I've known Jess since I was twenty-one and working my way through college (only child or not, my parents wanted me to make my own way). We worked at a grocery store close to campus and became fast friends back-stocking unwanted items one evening. We were inseparable after that—she'd drag me along to the local bars where I'd try to make myself invisible in a darkened booth while she drank and danced until the wee hours of the morning. We had standing Friday night dinner dates—basically anywhere she went, I followed.

While Jess may not be a large person physically, she makes up for it with a big personality and when I say Jess gets what Jess wants- I am not exaggerating in the slightest. With her bright blue eyes and dark brown hair, she stands out and men are putty in her hands. She wears her hair in whatever style is currently popular (at the moment she's rocking an asymmetrical bob and she may be the only person I know who can pull it off).

While she's most likely to be mistaken for a celebrity, I'm most likely to be mistaken for a librarian with my blonde hair pulled up into a bun and astigmatism that requires glasses on days I'm too lazy for contacts (almost every day). With her looks she could've had anyone, but Jess only goes after the "bad boys". You know the type; they show up late at night and leave before the sun comes up. They're never seen during the daytime (very similar to vampires).

While I find Jess's personality absolutely delightful, I am fairly certain that is not the reason they pay her visits late at night. However unlikely a pair we make, it works for us and I would trust her with my life.

She's there within an hour with the champagne I've requested. I don't know why, but champagne is really the only thing I like to drink. I adore it—the way the bubbles pop against your lips as you take a drink, it's like a little tickle—not that I would ever admit that to anyone. It's really the only highlight of attending weddings and showers, in my opinion.

She settles onto the loveseat as I sink back onto the floor. I'm feeling much more relaxed (buzzed) after a couple of glasses—it's a lot easier than I thought it would be to bring Jess up to speed on what's happened (*thanks alcohol*). She sits with wide eyes and her hand clapped over her mouth, completely in shock.

"Oh...oh Lizzie—I'm so sorry! I know that I'm going to break the friend code by saying this, but you know that I have never liked him. I'm not a bit surprised that the shit was cheating on you."

This was not news to me. The feelings of dislike were mutual between the two of them. Landon despised her lifestyle (*"Is there anyone in this town Jess hasn't slept with?"*) and she frequently complained that he was too rigid and uptight (*"Does he literally have a stick up his ass?"*). They've both got such strong personalities that I sometimes wonder how I fit in with either of them.

She gets up and goes through the entertainment center DVDs. "Let's find something funny to watch and take your mind off of everything and then later we'll find some of his stuff to destroy, okay? First things first though, wanna order a pizza?" I tell her I'm not really hungry. "When's the last time you ate something?"

I try to remember—"Maybe yesterday?"

Yeah, I'm pretty sure it was yesterday—unless wine counts as a meal. In that case, I'm getting five square meals a day.

"Geez, Lizzie. That's really unhealthy. You're eating tonight—end of discussion." She's so pushy.

We order a veggie pizza and crack open the second bottle of champagne while narrowing down our movie choices, eventually deciding on *Bridesmaids* (it's one of our favorites).

Towards the end, my phone chirps. I glance down and my heart skips, it's from Landon. Jess hits the pause button and leans over to see who it's from. "Do you want me to read it for you?"

"No, I'm good. Just give me a minute." I get up and go into the bedroom to read it. I sit down on the bed. Maybe he realizes this whole thing was a mistake.

"Hey— I wanted to let you know that I'll be by tomorrow evening to get some of my things. I'll call before I stop by. How are you?"

—Maybe not. I focus on deep even breaths as I re-read every word. I don't even know how to respond. "*How are you?*" What kind of question is that? What am I supposed to say to that? *I'm fine—thanks for wasting four years of my life?* I'm really not so sure that I'm the only one who needs therapy.

There's a knock at the door, "Lizzie, you okay? What'd he say?" I tell Jess to come in and hand my phone over. Her mouth moves silently as she reads the text, "What a tool! Why would he want to know how you're doing? —so that he and the home-wrecker can have a laugh at your expense? He's sick, sick I tell you!"

I shakily stand up and go into the bathroom where I begin splashing cold water on my face. Jess follows me in— "You don't look so good, girl. Why don't you sit for a second?" I shut off the water and sink to my knees in front of the toilet before emptying my stomach of alcohol and pizza. Jess grabs a washcloth and runs it under the faucet before

24

placing it on the back of my neck as my stomach continues its revolt.

CHAPTER THREE

Afterward, completely exhausted (mentally, physically, emotionally), I lay my face on the toilet seat and weep while Jess tries to comfort me. She insists upon staying the night and once she's made up her mind there's no use arguing. She puts the movie on in the bedroom and we lay next to each other—side by side, not saying a word as we finish it.

She's gone before I wake up the next morning, but she's left a note by the Keurig, *"Gone to the gym and then I'm gonna run home to change before work. I'll be back tonight—I have a work thing so it might be late. Text me when you're up. —J"* My head is pounding and my stomach is still uneasy so work is again out of the question.

I make myself a cup of strong black coffee and pick up my phone to text Lauren.

"Lauren—I'm still not feeling well so I won't be in today."

Within a minute she replies.

"Okay, I'm coming over there at lunch and you're going to tell me what's really going on."

I sigh before tossing my phone down. She'll probably fire me for this. A couple of years ago, she had appendicitis but refused to leave for the hospital until we saw all of our morning patients. She had the surgery and was back three days later. Girls like Lauren are machines; they don't let anything weaken or slow them down. Girls like her despise girls like me.

Lauren shows up right after noon with chicken noodle soup from a nearby deli. She takes one look at my face before dropping the deli bag on the counter and grabbing me in a rough hug. "Did someone die?"

I've never seen Lauren show any form of affection—you could knock me over with a feather right now.

I laugh bitterly before answering, "—Just my marriage."

Her eyes fill with tears and I'm taken aback because it's so not like her, "Elizabeth, please tell me what's going on. You're my friend. Let me help you."

I recount the story while she gets our soup ready and I find it's even easier to talk about it the second time. I manage to get through it without crying (I feel as though I'm telling a story about someone else's life) and she doesn't say anything at first. I don't think I've ever seen Lauren shocked speechless in all the years I've known her.

I brace myself for the harsh speech I'm bound to get at any moment though for shirking my work responsibilities, but it doesn't come and instead she whispers, "What are you going to do?"

"I-I don't know, Lauren. I really don't. I'm sorry I've left you stranded at work, but I can barely function."

"Stop—don't even think about work right now. I'm giving you the rest of the week off. You need to sort this out. I'll cover for you." She reaches across the table to grip my hand. I try to fight back the lump in my throat to no avail.

"Why are you doing this? I didn't think you liked me."

"I do like you, Elizabeth. I know I'm hard on you, but truth be told—you're my only friend. I know what is said about me behind my back and in spite of all of it you've always been so nice to me—even when I don't deserve it."

Lauren was a bit of a "ball-buster" around the office. When everyone reports to you, friends are in short supply. With the exception of me, no one wanted a close relationship with someone who had the power to fire them.

I try to let her words sink in. Besides Jess, I thought I was alone in this vast sea of people. Lauren is throwing me a lifeline and I grab on, just completely overwhelmed by it all.

She has to leave soon after to get back to work for the afternoon, but she promises to check in on me again after work. I hug her, feeling like it's such an inadequate way of expressing how I feel. "Lauren…Thank you for all of this— and for considering yourself my friend. I have a feeling I'm going to need as many of them as I can get if I want to get through this."

I spend the rest of the afternoon in bed (drinking the contents of yet another bottle of wine as the champagne is gone) and looking through our wedding photo album. I'm not reminiscing as much as looking for evidence of something I'd missed over the years. Katie is in nearly every photo and it's so glaringly obvious to me right now. There's a photo of her standing next to Landon at the bar, he's staring straight at the camera and she's staring at him (with what? — Lust? Longing?). In fact, she's got her eyes on him in nearly every photo. There's one of our first dance and she's in the background, glaring. How did I miss it? I guess I had blinders on and I truly thought Landon would never hurt me.

I wake up to a pounding on the front door and find that it's pitch black in the bedroom. How long have I been asleep? I stumble out of bed and realize belatedly that I am very intoxicated. How much did I drink? I make my way to the front door (using the walls for support) and throw it open to see—"Landon?"

"I've been calling you for the last two hours. I sent you several texts and you never responded. When you didn't answer, I thought you might be hurt." I look up in his eyes and it's obvious he's been drinking—quite heavily too judging from the smell of him.

"I'm sorry. I fell asleep." I notice that his eyes are no longer on mine and are instead roving downward over my body, taking me in. I look down and realize that I changed into another one of his shirts at some point, but I didn't bother buttoning it this time so my bra and panties are on full display in front of him (*thank God I actually put on matching underwear today*). He's staring at me, taking every inch in, and there's a hunger there. *Take that, Katie! Men love curves!* Before I can form a coherent response, he's kicking the door shut behind him and stalking towards me like I'm his prey.

I'm actually a little afraid of him right now, but desire is racing through me like a wildfire. Even in my addled state I know I need to kick him out, but I want him so badly. I want—no, I need him to comfort me. I should be asking him why he's here, but I don't know if I want to know the answer. I'm backing up away from him (albeit unsteadily), trying to gather my bearings when I realize my body is betraying me. I'm frightened, yet turned on by the man in front of me. My therapist is going to have a field day with this one.

He doesn't ask—in fact he doesn't say anything, just picks me up and carries me into the bedroom while taking my bottom lip into his mouth. I can feel how hard he is as my legs wrap around his waist and I moan, bringing my hands up to cup his face. He tosses me onto the bed and rips my lace panties off with one hand while the other takes a fistful of my hair in a death grip and I know that this isn't going to be sweet or slow. I open my mouth to stop him and he releases my lip long enough to slip his tongue inside, effectively silencing any argument from me. I don't know if it's the alcohol or him that's got me perched precariously on the edge, but I feel I am very close to falling off with him. He pauses for a second as he works to get his clothes off and I know that I can speak up and stop this before it goes too far. I remain silent.

I hear his belt buckle jingle as his pants fall to the floor. Then he opens the top drawer of his nightstand and gets a condom before his mouth is on me again as he picks me up and pushes me up against the bedroom wall, my legs wrapped around his waist. He stops his assault on my mouth and bites me on the neck before furiously entering me. His hands on my shoulders force him deeper inside me and then all coherent thought ceases and I let myself fall.

We sink down to the bedroom floor. I'm nestled against his chest, feathering kisses across his throat and listening to his heart race. *There's my husband, I knew he'd come back to me.* The anxiety has been banished back to its cave and I breathe easily. I'm beginning to drift off when he abruptly stands up and lays me back on the bed. He strips the condom off and sets it aside.

I stupidly think he wants to go for round two when he switches the bedside lamp on and I see his face. "Elizabeth, —God, Elizabeth—I'm sorry. I don't know what that was—I just saw you standing there half naked in my shirt and I didn't think." I sit up and wrap his shirt around me like a robe, suddenly feeling very exposed and raw as he begins putting his clothes back on. I manage to stutter, "I-I-I thought you were back. You wanted me. You can't deny what we are together. I'm your wife."

He puts his jeans back on and gives me such a look of pity that I want to claw his eyes out. "You think that was making love? Let's call it what it was—an itch that needed to be scratched. I'm still a man—you can't stick a barely dressed woman in front of me and expect me not to react. It shouldn't have happened and I'm sorry to confuse you, but I still love Katie."

I swallow the lump in my throat. I'm such a fool. "You u-us-used me—why?" I'm stumbling over my words in my fury and I can feel the tears forming—the anxiety perks its head up and makes its way out of the cave again. Landon backs up and sinks down to the floor next to the very same wall he just had me up against.

He has his head in his hands and even before he opens his mouth, I know what's going to come out. My gut churns from the stress. Like the pieces of a puzzle fitting together—now, I know why he's here and why he's drunk and I didn't think it was possible to hate him more than I did even just an hour ago—I was wrong. I've reached the threshold of hell.

CHAPTER FOUR

"Elizabeth," He can barely get the words out, "Katie's pregnant. She told me tonight and I'll be the first to admit that I freaked out. I had a few drinks—it was irresponsible of me to come here. You've already been through—" I don't even let him finish before I launch myself at him, screaming. I'm kicking, hitting, and scratching him as if my life depends on it—I want him to look on the outside like I feel on the inside. Of course, he stands a foot taller and outweighs me by a hundred pounds so my assault is short-lived before he has me pinned against the bedroom carpet. "Get off of me! Get your damn hands off of me." My screams have turned to sobs.

"What the hell is going on here?" Jess is standing in the doorway and I realize how this must look—me pinned again the carpet in just my bra and Landon's shirt with him on top of me. She turns to me, "The front door was unlocked. I heard you screaming," Then she unleashes her fury at him. "Get off of her before I call the cops and have you thrown in jail where you belong!"

He immediately releases me and backs up. I've managed to scratch the right side of his face, drawing blood. He looks wretched and I should feel some sense of victory, but I can tell by my labored breathing that I am spiraling down into an anxiety attack (I've lost). I sit up and lean against the bed, hugging myself as Jess comes over to me. The sobs wrack my entire body—I didn't think he could hurt me worse than he already had, but I've been cut open to the bone with this latest revelation. Jess is squeezing me so tight and I know she thinks she's helping, but she's making it harder to breathe.

I push her away and stand up. Landon is still there, leaning against the wall for support and he moves to come toward me. "Don't," I manage to choke out while holding my hands up, "—please don't touch me. You-you- promised me! You said we just needed to wait another month!"

There's a look in his eyes, disgust—Disappointment? But he knows what I'm referring to. We'd spent the last year talking about starting a family and every time it felt right, he pushed us back a month with various excuses.

"Landon, what did you promise her?" Jess is up on her feet and alert.

"Fuck, I just messed up. I screwed up everything. I never wanted to hurt you, Elizabeth. I swear to God I didn't!"

Landon's phone chirps at that point and he glances down at it before putting it back in his pocket. I know that it's Katie, I can tell by the expression on his face.

I turn to Jess, who is completely lost at this point, "Katie's pregnant, Jess." I stare at the carpet, willing it to swallow me whole. I sound so calm—completely the opposite of how I'm feeling. It's utterly silent in the room and I glance up to see her reaction; her eyes have widened and her mouth is hanging open. She closes it and I can see her jaw tighten. Yeah, she's going to kill him.

While she's laying into him, I slowly walk towards Landon's closet. I doubt they'll even notice I'm gone before it's too late. I know it's not rational, but the anxiety is roaring in my head and I can't take it anymore. I need some peace.

CHAPTER FIVE

I'm sitting on the couch in my therapist's office, while she sits across from me in her plush red velvet armchair, her legs tucked underneath her. Dr. White is in her mid-forties, but could pass for thirty-something easily. Her blonde hair, cut into a short bob, is always immaculate and her clothes are so trendy. I've dreamed of raiding her closet on more than one occasion. She takes a sip of hot tea before placing her mug on the small table next to her. She consults her notes before beginning,

"Elizabeth, we've been seeing each other for five years and in that time we've dealt with your anxiety, but your issues have always been manageable. We've made such progress and we both agreed that we could push our visits to once a month. So, I need you to walk me through this. What's changed? Why are we meeting three weeks early?"

I pick up a decorative pillow and hug it to my chest, my hands twisting the purple fringe. Dr. White sees that I'm using the pillow as a shield and notes it.

"Landon left me—I'm sorry, I thought by the third telling of this story that it would easier to talk about," She passes me the tissues and I dab furiously at my eyes before continuing. "He's been having an affair with his best friend's wife, Katie—the same Katie that I've been trying to convince to like me for four years. I found out when he left his phone in the living room with me and she sent him a text."

I pause and glance up at Dr. White taking notes. She nods for me to continue.

I recount the past three days for her, culminating in sex with Landon and the bombshell of Katie being pregnant, leading up to my panic attack, "The biggest arguments we had over the past year dealt with starting a family and now he's decided that he's on board, but not with me. It's so incredibly cruel. I just feel like I don't even know who I am anymore. He's taken everything from me—he won!' I spit the words out as if they leave a bad taste in my mouth and try fanning my eyes again to dry the tears.

"Elizabeth, what has Landon won?"

"Everything—he got me for four years and he had her on the side. Now, she's giving him a baby and I'm left with nothing. I gave him everything and what do I have to show for it?"

Dr. White just listens intently, never changing her facial expression. It's kind of a relief to talk about this mess without getting pitying looks. She makes a few more notes before breaking the silence.

"Let's talk about what you did the night he left. How did you cope?"

"I listened to music, cleaned the entire house, and cried—a lot."

"We've identified previously that you turn to cooking or cleaning as a coping mechanism when things get overwhelming, but I want you to look at your cleaning symbolically. Your husband leaves a pretty big stain upon your marriage. You scrubbing your home top to bottom—it's your brain's way of coping with this loss."

I look down at the pillow in my arms before answering, "I guess that's one way of looking at it, but it was a pretty crummy solution seeing as to how he's still gone and the stain's still there—which is why I'm sitting in front of you right now."

"Elizabeth, coping isn't necessarily meant to be a solution to our problems. It's just how we deal with tough situations—some people hit the gym and work out their frustrations, some people binge on comfort foods, and some people even turn to drugs and alcohol."

Her voice is so soothing—there's no hint of judgment. She just makes you feel like you're talking to a close friend. A close friend you pay by the hour, mind you, but a friend nonetheless.

"I'm really struggling to cope with my marriage falling apart. There's just this part of me that can't accept that he's gone. I think of how his friends and family must have reacted and it's like a knife to the heart. They hated me and I imagine they're all thrilled to know that I'm out of the picture now."

Dr. White takes a sip of her tea, "The night of the anxiety attack, when you felt yourself losing control, did you take any of your anxiety medication?"

"No, I sort of just let the rage and anxieties take over." Suddenly uncomfortable with where these questions are going, I chew on my lower lip and try to focus my attention on the large clock hanging on the wall behind her head.

Her office gives the impression that you've left Lubbock far behind and arrived in some faraway land with the warm colors on the walls, rich silk pillows, and ornate curtains. The lights are dim and there are candles burning on the table while classical music plays softly in the background. Everything in this room is calming. I'm so engrossed in taking in my surroundings that I don't hear her next question.

"I'm sorry—what?"

She gives me a bemused look, "I asked if you've taken any of your medication since Sunday night?"

I try to think back over the past few days before responding, "Oh…Um—no."

"In addition to what we've already discussed, have you been drinking to cope with this event or are you currently under the influence of alcohol or another substance?"

I cringe and let out a sigh, "Yes, I've been drinking basically since he left."

She notes my response, "Have you had any thoughts of harming yourself?"

Wow, she really knows how to make a person squirm. "The day after he left, I went into his closet because it smelled like him and while I was in there, I saw his gun collection. I'm not going to lie; a small part of me wondered what it would be like to put an end to this misery. It was just too much for me to deal with—but, the funny thing is that even though I'd contemplated some dark things the day after he left me, even I couldn't convince myself that he was worth it." I place my head into the pillow, weeping.

If she is shaken by my revelation, she hides it extremely well, "So you don't feel that it's something you would act on?"

"No—God no. Right after Landon left the pain was just unbearable—this crushing weight on my chest making it hard to breathe."

Dr. White leans forward in her chair, "What about now?"

I snort, "Now I just feel cheated—in every sense of the word. As little girls we're told by every movie we watch that our Prince Charming will come and save us from our ordinary lives. My Prince Charming saved me only to throw me over the side of a fucking cliff when I became an inconvenience." The tears start back up and I focus on a spot on the carpet, trying to compose myself.

"Okay, Elizabeth, I want you to do something for me. I think you need to stop drinking—alcohol is only going to intensify the dark feelings you're experiencing. I'm going to up your medication temporarily and I want you to promise me you'll take it. Also, I want to see you in my office once a week until you feel in control of this situation and these emotions. You have a lot of anger that we need to work through."

I'm still staring at the carpet, wrapping a tissue around my finger like a bandage. I begrudgingly admit, "You're right—I haven't even thought about my medication during this entire situation. I haven't thought of anything but what he's done to me."

She continues, "I also think it would be in your best interest to sever contact with Landon for the time being as he seems to be the biggest trigger in all of this and his behavior is destructive—,"

I know that she's right, but the thought of staying away from him seems impossible right now and it shows on my face. He's my drug of choice. Take away everything else, just leave him.

"I know that it's not a permanent solution, but until you're in a better spot emotionally—we can't take the chance of you relapsing. This latest encounter with him has just muddied the water. In the meantime, I want you to list your strengths and come up with some ideas for working through these negative emotions. Think of things you enjoyed doing before, write them down, and let's come up with things you can do for yourself when you feel an attack coming on."

I dab at my eyes and tell her that I agree.

She pauses before continuing. "Now, why don't you tell me what happened last night when you left Landon and Jess arguing?"

I know I should feel ashamed by what I've done and I try to force my expression to convey that, but it's no use. I can feel a smile starting before I even begin. I try biting my lip. "I went into Landon's closet and took a pair of scissors to every dress shirt and tie in there until he and Jess came in."

"And how did Landon react to that?" How she's able to keep a straight face is beyond me.

"Um, not well." That's the understatement of the year. He lost it—and made sure that every item of his was out of the house before he left. I don't think Jess's reaction helped matters much either. When they stumbled into the closet and found me, sitting in the floor, making fabric swatches out of his expensive work attire, Jess immediately fell against the door laughing. Like a small child being encouraged by a parent, I smiled up at her and continued cutting before Landon ripped the scissors from my hands, screaming, "What the fuck is wrong with you, Elizabeth? Are you insane?"

At this, she leans over and takes my hand. "You are so much more than this behavior and deep inside of you there is a strong woman waiting to rise up from the ashes."

After promising to be in her office the following Friday morning, I stand up and hug her goodbye. She stops me at the door, "Elizabeth, given the amount of stress you've been under, it wouldn't surprise me if you were trying to find a scenario or a way to change the outcome of all of this. I'm just not certain that destruction of personal property is your best solution." She laughs at the last part and ushers me out of her office.

Once I get home, I decide to allow myself until the end of the day to wallow in thoughts of Landon. Tomorrow will be a new start. I climb into bed and pull out my cell phone—it's time to listen to the three voicemails that he left the other night. I roll my shoulders and stretch my neck, like a boxer preparing for a match, before plucking up the courage to press play.

I check the time on the first message, 7:45 PM. His voice carries across the bedroom, invading every pore of my body, "Elizabeth, I never heard back from you yesterday. I'm still planning on coming by to get some of my things this evening. Call me back." Hmm…he sounds pretty sober so far.

Message number two came in at 8:16 PM.

"Elizabeth, I don't know if you're ignoring me, but I really need you to call me back and let me know if you'll be there to let me in. You know I left my garage door opener and key there Sunday night. Please call me." Okay, he sounds a little more desperate in that one, but still not drunk like I saw him when he was on my doorstep.

Message number three was sent at 10:08 PM.

"Baby (*baby?*), answer the phone please. I need you. I'm worried about you—[inaudible mumbling and crying]—I'm coming over right now." I exhale a breath I didn't realize I was holding. He called me a pet name, he's never done that before. I don't even want to think about how wasted he was or how he managed to make it to my house in one piece.

I press delete and the messages are gone—just like he is. I've just lost the one man who promised to love me until death and before I can even fully come to terms with that, he comes over and informs me that his mistress is pregnant.

Now he's gone, probably for good. Gone are the late night movie marathons together, the feel of him lying in bed next to me, his off-key singing in the shower...also gone are the disappointed looks, him berating me for not trying harder with his friends, anxiety attacks that occurred at inopportune times—is this what freedom feels like?

CHAPTER SIX

"Elizabeth, I really feel like we've made some progress this last month. You just seem more like yourself." Dr. White assesses me from her chair. I've been in her office once a week over the past four weeks. I've been taking my medication exactly as prescribed. She's right, I can feel myself coming out on the other side. Jess decided to move in with me and I think just having someone here has kept me grounded. I've also gone back to work and Lauren has been my rock while I'm there.

That's not to say I haven't had setbacks. It's still the first thing I think of when I wake up and the last thing I think about before I fall asleep, but the absolute crushing enormity of it all is lessening with each day. I have to remind myself that he isn't coming back and that it has nothing to do with me.

I experienced an aforementioned setback late one night. I was having trouble sleeping and decided to send some racy photos to Landon. I posed in my bra and panties along with the caption—"Do you see what you're missing? I bet Katie can't pull this off." I'll admit it wasn't my finest moment (I cringe even at the memory of it), but I was completely shocked when Jess walked in a few moments later. She confiscated my phone before informing me that she'd deleted Landon's number from my phone, adding her cell phone number to his contact.

She told me I'd get my phone back when I could make better decisions before yawning and heading for the door,

"By the way, from the photos it looks like you need to hit the gym with me tomorrow morning," she tossed the words over her shoulder and laughed as she made her way back to her bedroom.

In the entire time I'd been with Landon I'd lost touch with so many people that I used to call friends and the truth was that Jess was the only one who'd stuck with me through the good times and the absolutely gut-wrenching horrible times. Only a true friend would see a picture of you half-naked and not be afraid to tell you to get to a gym.

I decided to add early morning workouts to my list of strengths. And by "*I decided*" I mean that my new room-mate came in every morning at 5:30, switched on the bedroom lights, and refused to leave until I drug myself out of bed. I thought that Jillian from *The Biggest Loser* was a tough trainer—she had nothing on Jess Davis. By the second week of training with her, I found to my surprise that I didn't despise it as much. I hadn't made peace with the treadmill yet, but I actually found myself looking forward to the strength training. I've replaced drinking with exercise and I find that not only is the anxiety much easier to manage, but I'm more relaxed.

This continues until my doorbell rings one night. Jess is out on a date and I'm once again trying to catch up on *Glee*. I go to the door to find Mike, crying on my doorstep.

I let him in and he sits on the couch looking like a lost puppy. "She left me, Elizabeth. Katie left me today. She said she'd met someone and that she hadn't been happy for a while—and then she just walked out," he chokes up.

Oh no. She didn't even have the courtesy to tell him who she left him for? "I'm sorry to drop by unannounced, but I thought Landon might be here. I couldn't reach him on his cell, but I really need him to help me get through this."

He was really not up to speed on what was going on. I'd made no attempt to contact him in the days following my own abandonment. I guess I just figured Landon talked to him about us or that maybe Katie decided to come clean the same night I found out. I hadn't even had the courage to confront Katie, there was no way I was about to drop a bombshell on someone else's marriage (*weak, I know*).

I get up and walk into the kitchen. This was going to require a drink—for both of us. I find a couple of Heinekens in the back of the fridge (*I guess Landon didn't think to grab those*) and I carefully place his beer on a coaster in front of him before sitting back in my armchair with mine.

Mike and Landon grew up together. Even their mothers were close friends. Where Landon looked like an all-star quarterback; Mike looked like he belonged on a surfboard down by the Gulf.

He used to wear his blonde hair shaggy and had only recently begun keeping it cut above the ears. He stood about five inches shorter than Landon, and he was the quiet one between the two of them—but there was something about him that drew you in, like a moth to a flame. He could be so intense when speaking on a subject he was passionate about, but he was incredible low-key the rest of the time. He was incredibly handsome too and here I was— about to wreck his entire world with what I knew.

"Mike, there's a reason that Landon isn't here." He takes a sip of his beer and looks over at me, waiting on me to elaborate. I sigh and just like picking a scab, open my wounds up all over again.

He alternates between chugging his beer and putting his head in hands while I talk. Afterward, he just sits and stares at the fireplace, clenching and releasing his jaw. I don't know if I should go over and hug him or let him process everything for a minute—I choose to sit tight and fight back the waves of nausea caused by reliving these events.

"I've been with her for eight years—eight years—and now you're telling me that for four of those years I've been sharing her with my best friend? And now, she's having his baby?"

I nod, not entirely sure if he's really asking me or if it's a rhetorical question. He gets up and walks over to the fireplace, his hands holding onto the bricks for support. I silently will him to take deep breaths and to not break anything in his anger. "And how in the hell does she know it's his?"

Okay, that came out of left field. I throw my hand up in a 'wait' gesture, "I—you—what? Hold on, you mean you and Katie have been...um, intimate, recently?"

'Yeah, twice a week—nothing's changed in that department. So, you can see how I'd be a little thrown by her leaving."

I bring my hands up to my ears in a vain attempt to block the thought of them going at it from entering my mind. I don't know what to say. I push my glasses up and pinch the bridge of my nose.

He looks up at the large photo sitting on the mantle. It was taken on mine and Landon's wedding day—yeah, I haven't worked up to getting rid of mementos yet.

Afraid he's going to break it; I walk over and place my hand on his arm. He pulls me into him, holding me against his chest. It's strange to be held by him like this, but not entirely uncomfortable.

"How are you so strong in all of this, Elizabeth? I don't know how I'll ever recover from this. He was my best friend. If we were having problems in our marriages, we went to each other. And he used all of that information against me to get my wife into bed! Now, he thinks he can raise a child that could possibly be mine too?"

I wonder what kinds of things Landon went to him with. I imagine it went something like—*"My wife is a nutcase who suffers from anxiety attacks. I bet your wife doesn't do that, mind if I sleep with her?"*

Oh God, this situation is so messed up. It's like something you'd see in a *Lifetime* movie—*Her Husband's Best Friend and the Baby: a Story of Awkwardness and Paternity Tests.*

I try to pull away from his tight grip, "I'm not strong, Mike—just heavily medicated and seeing my therapist once a week to try to make sense of all of this. She should have her Mercedes paid off soon thanks to me." I'm trying to lighten the mood, but it's not working on him.

He holds me tighter and begins crying again and I feel myself on the verge of joining him as we share the same pain. Then he lays his head on my shoulder and moves his hands down my lower back—I stiffen. I'm right up against his hips and while he's mourning, it's obvious that his body is looking to forget things for a while. Are they all like this—or just the ones I'm running into lately?

I abruptly end the hug. "Mike, you should go."

He sinks down onto the ottoman and places his head in his hands again.

"I am trying to legitimately move on with my life and work through this and you think you can just put your hands

46

on me and what? What, Mike? You think I'm just going to sleep with you so you feel better?"

"Elizabeth, I'm sorry. You were just standing there in front of me and I didn't think it through. I'm just trying to process all of this."

"I'm getting really tired of hearing that. You think that just because I'm here that you're entitled to me. Well, guess what? I have feelings too and I'm struggling with this just as much as you are," I bite back a sob, "but you need to leave." I point to the front door and to my relief; he gets up and walks out, apologizing four more times. I slam the front door shut in frustration before leaning against it and breaking down—*so much for progress.*

CHAPTER SEVEN

Jess comes in a few minutes before midnight and calls out, "Well, that was a waste of four hours. Things were actually going pretty well—we had a lot in common, but then the check comes and he asked me to pay for everything because he goes on a lot of dates and it puts a real strain on his bank account!"

I laugh and turn down my Florence + the Machine radio station as she comes into the kitchen where I have the oven going and various pots bubbling away on the stovetop. She takes it all in and then walks into the living room as if looking for evidence. "He was here wasn't he?" Seeing my confusion, she elaborates. "Landon—he must've been here. The house is beyond spotless, you've got to be cooking for no less than fifty people over there, and you're listening to Florence— you're stressed or upset."

"Actually, Mike was here. Katie left him tonight," Jess rolls her eyes and fakes a gasp before climbing up on a bar stool at the island as I begin chopping vegetables.

"Yeah, I know—shocker. The kicker though? She just told him she met someone. That's it—no details. He came here looking for Landon. He had no idea, so I got the privilege of breaking the news to him."

"Do they think that he's too stupid to realize that Landon's new girlfriend looks a hell of a lot like his ex-wife? How were they planning on keeping that under wraps? So, you told him. How'd he take it?"

I begin layering the squash, zucchini, and onions in a baking dish with a little more force than is necessary, "He was angry, which I expected, but then he tried to put the moves on me when I went to comfort him."

"Wait, what? He tried something? So, did you, you know? —because I totally would have." She grins wickedly at me while doing what she thinks is a seductive wink, but gives me the impression that she's just had a stroke.

I swat her arm then sprinkle parmesan and pepper over the veggies before placing the dish in the oven and answering her, "No. I'm sorry to disappoint you. I kicked him out. If I'm going to be with someone else, I want it to be on my terms and not just because they're standing in my living room and they think it might help them feel better about themselves. You saw what happened with Landon. I don't want to feel like that again."

"Of course you don't, but you're not going to meet someone new staying cooped up in this house every evening. We need a girl's night—you and me versus every single man in this town."

As I wipe down the granite counters, I surprise her with my answer, "Yeah, I've thought about it and I think that's exactly what I need," Jess leans forward interested, "but I'm going to need a makeover first. If only I knew a hairdresser to help with part of that."

She jumps off of her barstool and comes over to me; she's in full hairdresser mode at this point and it's best to just sit back and let her sell me on her ideas, "What are you thinking you want—extensions? Yes, I am going to make you look so fabulous," seeing the wide-eyed worried look on my face she clarifies. "You'll look classy, I promise. We'll just lighten you up a bit and then give you a little length. You know I don't normally work Saturdays—being in such high demand during the week—but for you, I'm willing to make an exception," She grabs a wine glass and fills it, "Now that we've got that settled, I'm ready for my cooking lesson."

CHAPTER EIGHT

By lunchtime the next day, I'm unrecognizable. Gone is the sensible shoulder-length bob-and minus the lack of makeup and a sexy outfit, the girl staring back at me looks like she could take on the world. I stand up and hug Jess, my lip trembling as tears spring into my eyes. It's amazing what some highlights and hair extensions can do for one's image.

"Stop with the waterworks—you look amazing!" She has worked wonders once again—my own little hair savior.

I fan my eyes and smile at her, "How can I even begin to thank you? I know my face is now splotchy from crying, but I feel pretty for the first time in over a month."

Jess gives me a sly smile, "You can hand over Landon's credit card—because we're spending his money today," She cuts me off before I can voice an objection—"no arguing, Landon wants you to go buy a sexy little dress for our night out!"

We end up in a boutique dressing room, trying on dresses that are beyond expensive, and drinking the complimentary champagne like it's water. When I say complimentary, I mean that we went to the liquor store and purchased several mini bottles and smuggled them in to the boutique in our purses. The only thing missing from my "rock star experience" is a straw.

The dress I'm wearing at the moment is a slim black number with a plunging neckline. My curves could definitely work with this—not only do I feel sexy, but I look it. I turn the Italian designer tag over and nearly faint- $1560! I've never spent that much at one time on clothes; I mean my wedding gown was on a clearance rack at David's Bridal for crying out loud.

As I consider what I just spent on my hair and what I'm about to spend on a dress I intend to wear only one night-suddenly the champagne isn't settling so well. I manage to make it to the bathroom where I ever so gracefully puke in the sink. The bright side-I somehow manage to avoid ruining my dress in the process. Note to self, champagne on an empty stomach is a terrible idea— as is drinking as much as I have in the past twenty-four hours. I think about the repercussions of what I'm about to do as I wash my face with a damp paper towel.

There's no hope for reconciliation if I go through with this—like there had been much of one to begin with, what with all his talk of love and now a baby on the way. I've always played it safe and look where it's gotten me. No, I need this. Just one evening of recklessness to grieve the end of my marriage and then first thing tomorrow I'll go downtown and file. No sense in waiting for Landon to do it—no more helplessness. I must remember to Google "How to file for divorce in Texas" when I get home later. I've felt powerless in this situation. Maybe if I strike first with divorce papers I'll regain some sense of control. My inner romantic still holds out hope that if Landon can just see me all dolled up like this with another man paying attention to me; he might just change his mind—never mind the fact that he'd slept with me in the last month and had no qualms about leaving me all over again. What can I say? She's never been a realist.

There's a soft tap at the bathroom door. "Lizzie, is everything okay?"

I give my reflection a small nod as if finalizing everything. "Yes. I'm going to get the dress, but I'm going to need a pair of heels to go with it." I mean I did just throw up in their super-posh sink; I was kind of committed to buy something at this point.

CHAPTER NINE

It's a quarter to eight and I'm ready and waiting anxiously on the couch as Jess finishes getting ready in the other bathroom. Perhaps a little too anxiously, by the way my legs are shaking.

Yeah, men would certainly be falling all over themselves… to call me an ambulance…for the seizure I appeared to be having. Not exactly what I'd pictured in my head. You see, I have a bit of a confession to make. Landon is the only man I've ever been with romantically and (cough) intimately. When I say I gave him everything, I literally mean everything.

If I want to be reckless, I'm going to need to be relaxed and that's going to require a little extra pharmaceutical help.

Please understand I'm not looking for another relationship. Hell, I just want to be noticed tonight. I want some gorgeous man (or all of them) to look and me and see that Landon made a huge mistake. I go into my bathroom and take another Clonazepam.

I'm not a big fan of being under the influence of anything, as evidenced by the champagne event earlier in the day (and basically any of the other times I've had alcohol), but I also want to be able to let my hair down and enjoy myself in a crowded bar.

In the living room, I begin straightening the furniture and pillows, willing the medicine to kick in. Once that's done to my liking, I sit back down and wait for Jess.

"Oh my God, you look AMAZING! I knew you would!"
Jess is practically jumping up and down with excitement. She
looks absolutely stunning in a strapless turquoise dress and I
tell her as much. She looks amazing in almost anything she
puts on though—she could rock sweat-pants on a runway.
We climb into her bright red Camaro and head out.

"Jess, where are we going—to like a club?" She throws
back her head and laughs, a little too much if you ask me.

"Lizzie, you are absolutely adorable! It's been a while
since we've had girl's night though. Do you really want to
spend the evening with a ton of college kids?" I shake my
head, "Of course you don't. Seeing all those college girls will
just make you feel worse. I mean, you're thirty! We're fighting
gravity off more and more every day," seeing my horrified
expression she amends, "No, we're going to a nice bar where
you can meet people your own age. And unlike our clubbing
days, where you volunteered to be the designated driver every
single time, you're going to drink tonight."

While I'd expected us to be heading downtown, she takes
us to the south side of town. In between prestigious
neighborhoods and shops, there are several upscale bars
nestled in. There are no flashy signs; these bars pride
themselves on being classy and fitting in with the
neighborhood. We end up in front of one simply called
"Nick's." I have never been here, but Jess seems to think it
will do quite nicely.

We make our way through the crowded parking lot and
into the cool air conditioning. There's a popular country song
playing throughout the bar by George or Kenny, or—who
am I kidding? I prefer Broadway to Nashville, so I have no
idea. Jess confidently pushes through the crowd and makes it
up to the bar with me meekly following behind her, the

Clonazepam numbing me quite nicely. "What are you drinking?" She turns to look at me.

"Hmm, I'll have champagne?"

"Are you serious? And was your response a question?"

"Why, what's wrong with champagne?" I look down and begin fidgeting with my dress, embarrassed by my inability to even order a drink correctly.

"It's not a bad choice for a wedding or when you're home mourning the loss of your marriage, but it's not something you typically order at a bar. I forget you're not a big drinker though," she places a hand on my arm. "You're fine. I'll get us something; you go find us a table."

I find a booth tucked back into the corner. *So much for standing out.* Jess soon arrives with our drinks. "I got you a *Malibu* and pineapple. You'll like it. I promise".

I take a tentative sip and find the syrupy sweet liquid delicious. When she sees that I approve she raises her glass in a toast, "To Landon- may he get the karma that is most certainly coming to him. And to you, Lizzie, may you find that you are able to get over him by getting under someone else." I laugh as we clink glasses and she begins to scope out the possibilities.

An hour and several drinks later, I've still yet to find any prospects. Jess has managed to hand out her number to no less than six men. At the moment, there is a very interesting gentleman at our table proudly going over each tattoo he has and why he got them. I try to smile and nod at the appropriate times, but find my mind wandering.

I stand up a bit unsteadily, "I'm just going to run to the ladies room and then get some fresh air out on the patio."

"I'll just come with you," Jess attempts to get up.

"No, please stay. I won't be gone long." I make my way to the bathroom and pull out my cell phone while waiting in line. No text messages, but I have missed a phone call and there's a voicemail…from my mother. I've been avoiding seeing her since everything happened—faking illnesses, pretending I'm not home, lying and saying that I'd made other plans—you name it and she's probably heard it. I wince and press play.

"Sweetie, it's your mom. Listen, I heard the oddest rumor today. Your dad and I were getting groceries when we ran into Shirley. You remember Shirley; we play cards together once a month,"

Why do mothers do this? It's like if they don't explain how they know these people, we'll have no idea that they're referring to the friend they've had for forty years and assume it's someone new.

"Well, she said that she heard from her neighbor, Jean, that Landon has been seen without his wedding ring and with a woman who looks an awful lot like that Katie girl you two are friends with. I told her she was mistaken; that our Landon would never do that to you. I do hope you're being good to him. Anyway, call me back and let's get together for brunch on Sunday-the four of us. It's really been too long." I press delete and stare blankly at my phone until I'm nudged by the woman behind me, "It's your turn."

As I'm washing my hands a few minutes later, I wonder how in the hell I'm going to break the news to my parents. They adore Landon, a lot more than they ever have me. They've always doted on him for being so strong and not requiring medication and a therapist to get through everyday mishaps.

My mother actually called him up after he proposed and told him that no one would think unkindly of him if he decided not to go through with the wedding. As she put it, I had always been difficult to love and prone to dramatics with the temper tantrums (anxiety attacks) I threw. In my family, wanting to talk to a therapist about your feelings is equivalent to being a drama queen. If only I would choose to be happy, my life would be so much better; as if anyone would ever choose to live like this. I grab several paper towels to dry my hands and push the thoughts about what to say to my parents away. I'll deal with that tomorrow. Tonight is supposed to be about fun and forgetting.

I stop at the bar and order another drink—seriously, it's like liquid candy—before heading outside. The patio is not as crowded as it was inside and I immediately feel that I can breathe easier. I'll find a table and text Jess to meet me out here. This is much better. I see a table on the opposite side of the patio and I'm making my way across the deck to it when my heel slips in between the deck slats. My body is still moving forward, unaware that my right leg is not budging. I don't even have time to brace myself and I'm falling forward, drink and all. I hear someone yell, "Oh, heads up!" and a pair of strong arms grab me around the waist before I face plant onto the deck.

Unfortunately, my drink ends up all over him in the process. Realizing my foot is still caught in the deck; my rescuer leans down and manages to free it. "Are you okay?" His voice is deep with a strong southern twang and up until this moment; I've kept my head down, avoiding looking at him out of sheer embarrassment. "I-I-I'm fine. Thank you." I make eye contact as I thank him and- Oh my God, I've just been rescued by the hottest man ever. He reminds me of someone famous, but I can't quite place him in my semi-drunk state.

He smiles at me, "I think the only casualty was your drink-which I'm now wearing." His denim button up shirt is drenched in pineapple and rum, and is now clinging to what appears to be rock solid muscle. Stop staring. Look somewhere else. My eyes immediately move down to his tight-fitting jeans. Great, I am now staring at his dick- which also looks amazing, but is not helping my situation. I need to say something or else I'm going to look like a loon, "I'm so sorry about your shirt and falling on you. I'll let you get back to your evening. Again, I'm really sorry." I turn to walk away, mortified, and he grabs my hand.

"Wait, at least let me buy you another," at this he pulls his shirt up to smell it, "*Malibu* and pineapple?"

I grin at him, "Shouldn't I be buying you a drink?"

"Beautiful women should never have to buy drinks." At that, he leads me back into the bar with his hand on the small of my back. While shorter than Landon, he's still taller than me; I would guess he was close to six foot. His light brown hair is sun bleached and a little shaggier than I was used to seeing, but he pulled it off well. His skin is deeply tanned, so I'm assuming he must work outside for a living. He has some cross between a five o'clock shadow and a short beard. And his eyes, oh his eyes, are a deep shade of blue that mimicked my own. Once we reach the bar he leans into me so I can hear him over the crowd, "I'm David, by the way." He extends his hand for me to shake. I grin up at him (that's all I seemed capable of doing since I met him- grinning like a fool) and lean back into him, "David, I'm Elizabeth. It's a pleasure to meet you." And suddenly, I know exactly who he reminds me of. Landon was really into *The Walking Dead*—you know—the show about the zombie apocalypse. While it wasn't my top choice when it came to TV shows—I avoid the sci-fi genre if at all possible, I started watching it to humor Landon. I quickly found myself drawn in to the story and one character in particular. While he may not be wielding a cross-bow, I had most definitely just been rescued by Daryl Dixon. Be still my beating heart.

CHAPTER TEN

While he orders us drinks, I look around for Jess. Knowing her, she's probably off with tattoo boy letting him show her some of his more intimate ones. I shoot her a quick text,

"Met someone. We're on the patio if you need me."

David refuses to let me carry my drink, probably because he doesn't want to be wearing another one should I decide on a repeat of my earlier performance, and we make our way back onto the patio.

We find a secluded table in the corner and sit down. I glance over to where his friends are still enjoying their beers, "I hope I'm not keeping you from your friends. I don't want to monopolize your evening."

He chuckles and takes a sip of his beer, "Beth—can I call you Beth?" I nod, *honestly he can call me anything he wants* and he continues, "Beth, I see these guys several times a week. I was beginning to think that my evening was going to end up like it usually does; and then you literally fall into my lap, dumping your drink all over me in the process. Now I'm sitting here wanting to know where you've been hiding all my life— Sorry," At this he stands up and unbuttons his shirt, pulling it free from his jeans and laying it on the chair next to him before sitting back down in a white sleeveless under-shirt that leaves nothing to the imagination. Fuck me, the man is made of rock-solid muscle.

"I'll let that dry out a bit." It's like there's some magnetic pull between us and I can't look away. His body says that he is no stranger to hard labor and he has several tattoos down his arms and across his chest. Unlike tattoo boy, it only enhances his good looks.

I wonder if people often mistake him for looking like Daryl Dixon, not that I would ask him that. That would be weir—"So, do you ever get told that you look like Daryl Dixon from *The Walking Dead*"? I clap my hand over my mouth, horrified. *Why did I just say that? I'm blaming the rum for this one.*

He laughs and I swear I could listen to that all day— such a rich, guttural sound. "I love that show. You mean Norman Reedus though, I'm assuming—Yeah, every once in a while someone mentions the resemblance. I don't see it though." I nod while taking a long drink to keep my mouth quiet—*just keep sucking on the straw.*

It's no use. "No, I meant Daryl Dixon. Norman Reedus looks pretty clean-shaven compared to you. It's like maybe you've spent the day hunting zombies before coming in to have a beer and rest," His face falls at this and I realize what I've just said. "N-n-no, I don't mean that you're not absolutely stunning" —*Oh my God! Why? Why am I still talking?* "You are incredibly hot. Look at Daryl, he looks pretty worn down most of the time, but women everywhere would drop their panties in a heartbeat." I put my head down. *Yeah, this is why I've been with one man my entire life.* I'm thirty years old and I cannot have a normal conversation with a man without insulting him or telling him I want to drop my panties in the process. I cringe and glance over, expecting him to get up and run from me. Instead, he looks bemused. He takes another long swig of beer, "So, I make you want to drop your panties? That's not necessarily a bad thing." He winks at me and it's like white hot heat quickly making its way south. I am extremely turned on right now.

I protest, "This stuff is like truth serum!" This elicits another hold nothing back kind of laugh from him, "In that case, I'd better get you another one."

We continue with the playful back and forth banter as we play twenty questions with each other. David is thirty eight and grew up in south Texas. He does construction for a living—that explains the tan, has never been married, and has no kids.

As he begins to ask me questions, I decide that I will play it cool. *Yeah, not too many details—that scares men off,*

"I'm thirty, mainly grew up here, and up until a month ago was happily married for four years. Turns out, my husband was having an affair with his best friend's wife for literally the entire time I've known him. We don't have any kids because he was never ready; which is ironic, because the home-wrecker is now pregnant,"

I down the rest of my drink in shame, "—this is why I don't drink. It's like every thought in my head is now making its way out of my mouth. I'm sorry." David looks a little taken aback and really who wouldn't be with that kind of introduction.

I'm waiting to hear the scrape of his chair legs against the deck as he tries to get as far away from me as possible. To my surprise, he leans over and places his hand over mine, "You're beautiful and downright funny even though it's obvious you don't mean to be. If he can't see what's right in front of him, well then fuck him…" I interrupt by leaning into him, placing my hands on either side of his face, and pressing my mouth to his.

Kissing him is electricity and fireworks and everything you see in movies. I didn't expect that. I was just following my impulse. His hands come up and he's running his fingers up and down my arm creating electric shocks that leave me wet and wanting him. This is chemistry, pure and simple.

We pull apart a few minutes (*hours?*) later to hear his buddies cheering him on. I blush and self-consciously tuck my hair behind my ears. His look mirrors my feelings. He pulls me closer and whispers in my ear, "Do you want to get out of here?"

I feel him smile as I breathlessly answer, "Yes, let me just go tell my friend that I'm leaving." He asked me—a man finally stopped to ask me if I want to do something instead of just assuming.

I shakily stand up and I'm not sure whether it's him or the alcohol that's got me so off balance. He stands up as well and pulls me in for another kiss, his hands holding tightly to my waist. "I'll be waiting right here for you."

He sits back down and I give him a small wave as I turn to head back inside. This is so unlike me- I love it. I did something reckless and it's paying off. I'm doing cartwheels inside and my inner romantic is lighting candles and chilling the champagne. *If sex is anything like kissing him, I'm a goner.*

I'm so caught up in this feeling that it takes me a second to realize that I've got tunnel vision. I am incredibly dizzy and as I turn to grab a chair my legs give out, my head making a terrible sound as it bounces off the wrought iron table.

I can feel warmth down the right side of my face, but I'm incapable of doing anything to stop it. I should've known better than to drink that much—looks like my rock star lifestyle has finally caught up with me. The last thing I see before blacking out entirely is David standing over me, shouting my name and calling for help.

PART TWO: FALLING

CHAPTER ELEVEN

The bright sunlight pierces the back of my eyelids like daggers, trying to force them open. I struggle with consciousness; my head hurts so badly. I'm definitely hung over. It takes a minute for the blurred images to become my surroundings—*where are my contacts?* and I realize that I have no idea where I am. The room is all white—*Am I dead?* I can hear a hissing sound coming from my face and I tentatively reach my left hand up, touching a tube running under my nose. I'm on oxygen.

Oh my God, how much did I drink last night? I check my hand and find there's an IV port. I'm in a hospital bed, but why? I remember drinking with Jess and meeting someone—David. And I was supposed to go home with him, but I fell. I was bleeding. I never told Jess where I was going. I stiffen as I feel movement beside me. *Okay, don't panic. Someone is lying next to you in this bed.* I turn to the right and see David curled up on his side, his right arm draped across my abdomen. Well, he looks like hell. We definitely drank too much.

I gently nudge him, "David," my voice sounds so raspy, "wake up." He jerks awake so suddenly that he almost falls off the tiny bed. "Oh, thank God, you're awake," he rolls out of the bed and heads for the door. "Let me just grab a nurse."

He rushes out of the room and comes back with a heavily pregnant blonde nurse. She starts to check my vitals. "Good morning, we're so glad you're awake. You gave us all quite a scare," I nod slowly at her as she places the blood pressure cuff on my arm. "Do you remember anything about how you got here?"

I take a deep breath and sigh, "Yeah, I drank too much and fell, hitting my head." I see looks of confusion on both of their faces.

"Okay, I'm going to grab your doctor. Just sit tight." She leaves the room and returns a few moments later with an older man.

"Hello, Elizabeth, I'm Dr. Briggs and I'm going to ask you a few questions to evaluate your brain function," He's a very handsome man with green eyes and salt & pepper hair. I'd guess him to be in his mid to late fifties. He consults a clipboard before beginning. "What is your full name?"

"Elizabeth Marie Scott." I hear David make a sound of surprise beside me, but the doctor holds his finger up as if to silence him. He notes my response on his clipboard.

"When were you born?"

"December 5, 1983"

"Where were you born?"

"Fort Worth, Texas"

"Do you know what city you are in now?"

"Lubbock."

He jots this down before continuing, "What is the last event you can recall from before the accident?"

"Last night, I went out to a bar with my friend, Jess, and I met David," I gesture towards him, "I was going to tell Jess that I was leaving and I felt dizzy. I reached out for something to steady myself, but I fell and hit my head on a table." David stands up at this, seemingly upset.

Dr. Briggs turns to the nurse, "Kassie, why don't you take David down to get some coffee while we finish up here," She

70

nods and leads him out of the room. "Okay, Elizabeth, let's continue. Do you know what time it is now?"

I glance around the room for a clock and not finding one, answer as best I can, "Morning time?" He smiles at me as he records my answer.

"Do you know what day of the week it is?"

"Um, Sunday?"

"Do you know the month?"

"It's June."

"What year is it?"

"2014"

"Are you married?"

"Yes, to Landon Scott."

"Do you have any children?"

"No."

"Okay, we're going to stop there for a bit and let you rest. I'm going to order some lab work and I'd like to do another MRI and CT scan as well." He gets up to leave.

"Wait, Dr. Briggs—what happened to me?"

"Elizabeth, you and your husband were involved in a car accident and you were brought in with a head injury. You've been unconscious for three days. There were a few brief periods where you appeared to be on the verge of waking up, but this is the most conscious you've been."

I start at this revelation, "My husband? Is he okay? What happened?"

He pats me gently on the arm. "Why don't you just rest now and we'll work some more later."

Landon's dead and they don't know how to break it to me. Now my parents have yet another reason to hate me. I probably drove us into oncoming traffic. That bastard was probably telling me that he and Katie wanted to name their unborn child after me to show that there were no hard feelings.

Before he can leave, David and Kassie come back into the room. David's holding a Styrofoam cup of black coffee and he opens his mouth as if to say something. Dr. Briggs stops him, "Okay, Elizabeth, I want you to get some rest and David; I'd like to speak to you out in the hallway."

Before I can say anything else, they leave me alone with Kassie. I can hear them arguing outside the hospital room door, unfortunately they're doing it a little too quietly for me to hear anything.

Maybe if I could just get up, I could get closer to the door and find out what they're so tersely discussing. I press the up arrow on the bed panel and try to sit up, but the shooting pain in my head forces me back down. "Elizabeth, let's take it easy. There's no need to rush. I'll incline your bed a little more and we'll get you used to sitting up a step at a time." I start picking at my fingernails—a nervous habit while studying the tubes coming out of my hand when I notice my hospital bracelet:

Greene, Elizabeth Marie
12/05/1983 30 F

That's not my last name. There's been a mix up and that's why everyone is freaking out. It still doesn't explain why David's here though. It feels like my throat is closing and I can't breathe. I need to get out of here.

"Nurse—Kassie, this isn't the right last name. My last name is Scott." She tries to calm me down and recline my bed back, but I'm having none of that.

"I have to get out of here. I'm not supposed to be here. Listen to me! There's been a mistake because that's not my name!"

CHAPTER TWELVE

"Elizabeth, just lie back and relax. You've gone through a lot and I don't think you're quite ready to be up and moving around just yet. Just breathe—in and out."

Her attempts to comfort me are just irritating me further. I really have no idea what is happening and I just want to throw something. I grab the only thing I can find—the remote/call button device and fling it at Kassie's head. Luckily, the cord is wrapped around the bed and it doesn't even come close to hitting her.

Oh my God. I just tried to hit a pregnant woman! Who am I? I am never violent. "Kassie, I am so sorry! I don't know what came over me. I swear I'm not like that!" Great, here come the waterworks. This is not going to help my headache at all. Surprisingly, she pats my hand calmly, and tells me she'll be back soon. She's probably about to phone the psych ward.

I hear the door open and then David is by my side, comforting me. The nurse walks over to the door to leave, "Mr. Greene, I'm going to visit with Dr. Briggs and see when he wants us to run those scans." Did she just say Mr. Greene? "That nurse just called you Mr. Greene and that's the name on my bracelet. Is this a joke?" I'm getting so frustrated by the lack of information being given here, "Please just tell me what the fuck is going on!" Wow, now I'm speaking like a sailor. Not only am I frightening nurses, but I'm scaring myself now too.

David gets up and starts pacing, "Beth, please relax," he lowers his voice and points at the door. "Dr. Briggs doesn't think it's a good idea to overwhelm you with a lot of information right now, but I can't take this! We have the same last name because," he breaks down as he says this and sinks into a nearby chair, his hands on his head, "we're married, okay?"

I swallow. I need to play this cool or I will certainly be in straight jacket before the day is over, "What—how long have we been together?"

"We've been together five years—married for four."

"Do we have children?"

"No, we've been trying, but um," he swallows, "it just hasn't happened yet."

"Was I married before?"

He shoots me a puzzled look, "Uh, no—it's just been me."

I have a million questions I need to ask him, but I just don't know where to start. I want to know if we're happy, how we met, and obviously I want to know if he's ever cheated on me with someone named Katie. I mean, just to be on the safe side.

We sit in silence, each of us lost in our own thoughts. I take some time to study him while he stares out of the window. Whereas he looked so confident and put-together last night— or whenever that was, he now looks haggard. His shaggy hair is in desperate need of a wash, he has dark circles under his eyes like he hasn't slept in days, and what was a five o'clock shadow is now definitely moving into beard territory. I take him in and find him still incredibly sexy. He's twisting a napkin in his hands—*it looks like I'm not the only one with nervous habits*, a simple gold band adorning his left ring finger. He's got bruises and scratches down his right arm.

"What happened to your arm?"

He stops wringing the napkin and glances at his arm before looking at me, "I got a little banged up in the car wreck. Just a few bumps and bruises, it's nothing to worry about. You're the one I'm worried about." He smiles as if to reassure me that all is fine with him.

"What happened to us? How did we get into an accident?"

"The people in this town drive like idiots. You do remember that, right?" I nod at him and we both smile because that is an entirely accurate assessment of ninety percent of the drivers here.

"Well, we were heading back home after dinner and we got to that intersection over by Slide Road and this teenager was texting while driving. He never saw that the light was red and he ran it—t-boning us on the passenger side.

"Here I was, trying to get you out of the car and he was just standing there mumbling over and over about how sorry he was and how he was just trying to text his girlfriend that he was almost to her house." David slams his left fist down on the arm of the chair and stands up, pacing again.

"I thought he killed you," he sobs. "You wouldn't answer me and your eyes- they were just wide open- staring at nothing. There was so much blood and I thought I'd lost you. I was just filled with this rage. Had the emergency crews not shown up, I don't want to think about what I would've done to that kid."

His grief is overwhelming me and I just want to hold him until he calms down. I pat the bed in a gesture for him to sit down next to me. He sits down and I reach for his hand.

The air is suddenly popping with electricity, *at least we still have that*, and I find myself wanting to get to know him better. I'm completely in lust with him, but could I love him? As he brings my hand up to his mouth to kiss it —such a simple gesture; I think that maybe I could—that, and the realization that my other spouse appears to be imaginary.

I want to put a smile on his face so I use my free hand and beckon him closer. As he leans down over me I whisper in his ear, "David," I can tell he's smiling, "you really need to shower." He laughs and kisses me on the nose before standing up again.

"Beth, it's like you're already on your way back."

CHAPTER THIRTEEN

Kassie and a male nurse come in to take me for more testing. He introduces himself as Tony and they work on getting me out of bed and into a wheelchair. She takes me off of the oxygen, while he gathers my IV pole and catheter bag—I'm already thinking of ways to hide that from David, who's on the other side of the bed.

Kassie presses the incline button on my bed until I am fully sitting up. "Okay, Elizabeth, we're going to get you into a wheelchair and all I need you to do is put your arm around Tony. I would normally be the one helping you but," she gestures to her swollen belly and then looks over to David. "I want you to go over there and help Tony with her legs and I'll get behind her." As I drape my left arm across Tony's shoulder, he gently leans back until I am in a sitting position. David brings my legs over until they're dangling off the edge of the bed. Kassie is still holding on to me from behind. "Okay, let's rest for a second. How do you feel?"

I nod, "Good."

"Alright, let's have you plant your feet on the floor with you still holding on to Tony and we'll get you in the wheelchair." As I place my feet on the floor, gravity helps me slide off the bed. Tony warns me to take it slow as I rise up to a standing position. As I do, I feel a cool breeze down my backside and even before I can say anything David pulls my gown closed. He laughingly whispers in my ear, "Let's not give Tony a show," before both men get me into the wheelchair. He gives me a quick kiss on the cheek before they wheel me away, promising to take a shower while I'm gone.

After the CAT scan, I'm taken for an MRI. I feel my heart rate pick up at the thought of being inside of a narrow tube for forty-five minutes and try to focus on my breathing to calm down. Thankfully, my doctor agrees to sedate me beforehand.

The nurse tech explains that they're going to give me ear plugs and that the test will be broken into two parts, "After the first portion, we'll bring you out and inject contrast through your IV; then we'll begin the second portion. If you'll just keep your eyes closed from start to finish, it'll help with claustrophobia."

I nod nervously at him and continue taking deep breaths. Another nurse injects the sedative into my IV port as the tech puts the ear plugs in and then attaches what feels like vise to hold my head straight. Once he places the cage over my face he signals that I should close my eyes. Then he slides me in.

The medicine begins working within minutes and takes the edge off. *Holy shit, this machine is loud. I wish David were here.* The thought is so sudden and takes me by surprise. I decide to pass the time spent laying here by exploring this further. I didn't wish for Landon—not that it would do me a lot of good to wish for someone who may or may not exist. I feel like I should be sad or more freaked out, but my previous marriage ended up being such a joke that I find myself not entirely upset at my circumstances. I just wish I knew how I ended up here with all these memories, but no recollection of David other than what appears to be our initial meeting.

David is the polar opposite of Landon. Landon couldn't even stand to be around me when I was sick. He'd encourage me to get up and shower, maybe try some make-up and see if I didn't feel better. Make-up is the cure for colds and stomach viruses, everyone knows that. David seems genuine. I feel like I've seen him show more emotion in a day than Landon did in four years. He didn't seem disgusted helping me out of bed, quite the opposite really. The way he held my gown closed—there was possessiveness there. It feels so good to be wanted. I don't know if the thing with Landon was just some crazy dream or a psychotic episode. I really hope it's the former or I may save everyone else the trouble and check myself in at the psych ward.

David said I wasn't married to anyone before and I believe him. There's just so much to process—I went from trying to pick up the pieces of my marriage to being thrust into another one entirely.

Just like being caught up in a typical west Texas sandstorm, you can't see your hand in front of your face. It's the same way inside my head right now. Random thoughts and memories swirl violently and I find that I'm unable to grasp onto anything that would give some clue about my present life.

At this point, the technician slides me out of the MRI tube to inject the contrast and I give my mind a momentary break. I assure the technician that I'm okay before I'm put back in. *I wonder how David is in bed.* Oh wow, there's yet another random thought. My inner romantic pops her head up, interested.

Thank the Lord that my face is hidden as I'm sure it's bright red. I suppose it is a normal thought to have about one's husband. *Most women know what their husband is like in bed. Right.* I guess I just didn't think about it much with Landon—*if he even existed.* This is so out of character. If someone were to describe me before, they'd use words like meek, submissive, and unsure. I feel like I can't relate to that woman right now.

Something's been born in me through this accident, some confidence that's building. I felt the stirrings in my previous life after my imaginary husband left me—*Well, what else am I supposed to think without any concrete evidence?*, but this feels solid—permanent. This could be my second chance. I need to let go of the past, at least what I remember as the past, and embrace my new life, but I'm so confused. Did I invent a person in my head—is the brain even capable of that?

I remember seeing a special on TV awhile back that dealt with dreaming of seemingly unknown people. Scientists discovered that the dreamers had actually encountered these "unknown people" in their daily lives. While they didn't remember, the brain stored the image of the other person's face. *That's frightening.*

What if it's too good to be true? Do good people actually get the life they deserve? I don't want to let my inner cynic run free, but I can't let naiveté rule either. I need to be cautious—this isn't a *Disney* movie. If only something made sense.

They wheel me back to my room afterwards and there's David, all cleaned up—except for the blood stained clothing he's still inexplicably wearing. He catches me looking, "I didn't bring a change of clothes. I was afraid if I left you right after the accident, I'd miss you waking up."

I nod dumbly at him, the drugs still in full effect. I'm feeling a little sleepy at the moment and find myself dozing off the minute my head touches the pillow. The next few hours are filled with fitful sleep. I dream that I'm trying to get into a locked room. My fists are bloody from pounding on the heavy wooden door. No matter what I do, the room remains locked. I wake, covered in sweat.

David sees that I'm fully awake and fishes my glasses out of my purse for me.

"Thank you—and thank you for staying. You know, I've been trying to come up with ways you could help me remember our life together. Do you have your cell phone? There's bound to be pictures of us on there. Maybe it could help." He reaches into his back pocket and pulls it out; then he punches his security code in and hands it to me. He settles back into a chair and props his feet up on the bed beside me.

I look down at the phone background and it's a picture of us on what looks like a beach. I hold up the phone to show him, "Where are we here?"

"Cabo San Lucas. I surprised you for our anniversary with that trip. We stayed at this all-inclusive resort right on the beach and we took a glass bottom boat tour one day. At night they would build a big bonfire on the beach and play live music. Trust me; we had a lot of fun that week." He smiles and gives me a wink and I feel a jolt of longing. Even though my mind cannot remember a life with him, my body seems ready to do just that. My inner romantic is batting her eyes like a Hollywood starlet.

I go back to the phone and hit the photo icon. He has over sixteen hundred photos—impressive. I choose camera roll and scroll to the top, trying not to pay attention to what I'm seeing. I want to start at the beginning and work my way down, no cheating—that's my OCD side coming out. The first photo is of me holding a rose between my teeth. I look ridiculous, but happy. He moves his chair so he can see what I'm seeing. "That was at my cousin's wedding two years ago."

"Why is my face so shiny?"

"It was an outdoor wedding in Louisiana in July. I thought we were going to melt—it was so humid!"

There are so many pictures of us in various places: drinking green beer on St. Patrick's Day with shamrock stickers on our faces, me using a sparkler as a fairy wand on the fourth of July, making our goofiest faces for whoever was holding the camera (tongues out and eyes crossed)—Landon and I never did these things. Everything with him was formal compared to this. I have never seen myself look so happy.

David interrupts my thoughts by taking the phone from me. "I just thought of something," he clicks the music icon and scrolls down to the song he wants, "it's not country, but you love this song so I made an exception." Suddenly Jason Mraz's voice comes pouring out of the phone's speaker. Wait a minute, I know this, "I won't give up—it's a beautiful song. I do love it." He squeezes my hand, "It reminds me of us, with everything that's going on." He leans over me and I know exactly what he's about to do and I find myself trying to sit up and meet him halfway. Before our lips can connect, the nurse comes back in. We immediately pull apart like two jumpy teenagers and shut the music off.

Kassie pretends not to notice, "Elizabeth, we'd like to try to get you cleaned up. Would you like to try to get up and take a shower?" I nod at her as she checks my vitals. I've still yet to see myself in a mirror, but I assume I need a good scrubbing.

I'm suddenly a bit self-conscious about how I must look and I put my head down and start picking at my fingernails again. David speaks up, "You know you look incredible right now, right?" I blush furiously as we're not the only people in the room and ask incredulously, "Really?"

Kassie finishes taking my vitals (other than my heart rate being elevated, I'm good) and enters her notes on the computer before turning back to me. "Okay, I'll go start the shower. Sometimes, it takes a while for the water to heat up."

David waits to answer me until we hear the water kick on. "Yeah, Beth I really think you look beautiful. Hell, I've spent the last three days worried sick about you and now that you're awake and okay I can't stop thinking about kissing you and running my hands all over your body. How's that for an insight into the male mind?"

I don't even think before answering, "It might help me remember." His eyes widen with shock—*and lust. There is a healthy amount of lust in the look he's giving me*, and I realize what I've just told him. I basically just told a complete stranger I wanted to have sex with him. The old Elizabeth would have never been so bold. My inner romantic is about to swoon from all the sexual tension in this room and is fanning herself dramatically. I've never felt so empowered.

Kassie walks back in, "Okay Elizabeth, let's get you undressed and all cleaned up." I suddenly realize what that will imply and shoot her a panicked look—all empowerment is now gone and my inner romantic is placing her head in her hands, ashamed. David notices my face and speaks up, 'I was just going to head down to the cafeteria and grab some lunch—you want anything, Beth?" I tell him I'm fine and breathe a sigh of relief. He moves to kiss the top of my head and in my desire I reach up and pull his mouth down over mine.

If I thought the first time we kissed was like fireworks, this must be "Shock and Awe." I've never been kissed like this man kisses me. We pull away, I almost expect to see actual sparks, and I mouth the words "thank you" to him. My heart feels as though it could beat out of my chest and when David stands up to leave, I'm aware of just how much of an effect I have on him. He tries to adjust his jeans discreetly before slipping past Kassie and out of the room. My inner romantic is already digging through the lingerie drawer and I find myself a little frightened by how much I already feel for this man.

CHAPTER FOURTEEN

As Kassie helps me out of my gown while gathering up all the various tubes running out of me; I study myself in the mirror. My right eye is black and blue and I have some stitches (they're small lacerations, probably caused by flying glass) around my hairline and down the right side of my face. Facial cuts can bleed so much though; I can see how David would've been scared. There is an enormous black bruise running from my right shoulder to my left hip from the safety belt and I'm pretty sure several of my ribs are cracked, but overall, I look pretty much the same as I always have—just slightly more banged up.

Kassie puts a plastic bag over my IV hand to keep it dry and then helps me get situated on the bench sitting inside the shower. She gives me the hand-held shower head and I sit, letting the warm water cascade down my body. A hot shower is right up there with heated blankets in my book of creature comforts. After helping me wash my hair, Kassie hands me a soapy washcloth to get the rest of my body (they really do not pay nurses enough).

We haven't really spoken much up until this point when I break the silence as she's helping me dry off. "How far along are you?"

She pauses in her drying to answer me, "I've got about eight weeks left."

"Boy or girl?"

"Boy." She goes back to drying me off taking extra care to not bump any tubes in the process.

"Kassie—I'm really sorry about earlier. That's not me. I don't make a habit of throwing things, please know that. I'm just so confused by all of this, but that is no excuse for what I did."

She nods while listening to me, "I understand how lost you must feel and I do forgive you. It's not the worst I've ever seen a patient behave. You know—your husband is a good man. I've seen a lot of men come through here with a girlfriend or spouse and the majority of them can't handle the stress of seeing someone they love in pain. He didn't leave your side once—not even to eat something. Several nurses and I just started bringing him a tray so he'd get something," I bite my lower lip and blink rapidly to keep from crying in front of her again, "All he's done is sit and hold your hand or lie next to you in that bed. I know you don't remember and you're frustrated, but it's pretty obvious to everyone around here how much he loves you."

I thank her and continue trying to fight back tears. She smiles at me and I can tell she's on the verge of tearing up as well by the way her lower lip is trembling, "Okay, Elizabeth. Let's get you dressed and get that catheter out—before we're both crying." I dab my eyes and smirk at her, "Well Kassie, catheter talk is one way to get someone to stop crying," before we both dissolve into laughter.

Twenty minutes later, I am catheter free and sitting in a new gown on clean bed sheets. There's a knock at the door and in walks Jess. "Jess—Oh my goodness, you're real!" She cocks her head to the side and gives me a sympathetic smile before coming over and enveloping me in a tight hug.

"Oh Lizzie, it's me—in the flesh. David told me you were awake, but when he explained that you didn't know who he was—" she falls apart and it takes a minute before she can continue, "I was so afraid you wouldn't recognize me! I'm sorry to drop in on you, but once I heard you were up I asked David if he'd mind me having a little one-on-one time with you." I notice she's holding a duffel bag.

I point to it. "What's the bag for? Are you moving in again?" I laugh, but it's obvious she has no idea what I'm referring to. This is going to take some getting used to.

"Well, I went out and grabbed a few things I thought you might like. And you know me; I can't let you go around with bad hair. What would people think?"

She sets the bag down next to me on the bed and I begin going through it. There is a pair of pajamas, some face wash, make-up, and gossip magazines. She gestures to the items, "I think the make-up is close to what you wear and the magazines are reading material while I fix your hair."

I give her another squeeze and she begins plugging various beauty appliances in to outlets. "So, where did David go?"

"Oh, I told him to take some time to himself—maybe go grab a change of clothes while I helped you get ready. He can't really pull off the blood-stained look. Plus, it gives us a chance to have some girl talk."

"Daryl Dixon can pull that look off. He can pull anything off." I grin before realizing I've spoken the words aloud. *Seriously, is the filter between my brain and mouth broken?*

"Oh Lizzie, you and your *Walking Dead* references—I get it. David does look like one of the main characters, but you're still not going to convince me to watch it. I don't do creepy."

At least I'm not the only one who sees the resemblance. "So, I really am married to him?"

"Yes ma'am—every girl's fantasy is to marry a bad boy and turn him into the boy next door—or maybe it was just mine."

"So, you're saying he was a 'bad boy' when I met him?"

"No, let me explain. He's always treated you like a queen. I just remember when you first introduced me to him and I thought he seemed more likely to belong in a biker bar than with you. I just worried you would get your heart broken. I thought he was more my type. Looks can be deceiving though, yeah?"

She has no idea how true that it. People always talked about how perfect Landon and I were together (Jess never did, but she and Landon were never going to see eye to eye on anything)—little does anyone ever fully know what goes on behind closed doors. Speaking of—"Jess, did I ever date a Landon Scott?"

She pauses, "Not that I recall. No, that name doesn't ring a bell."

She wraps a section of my hair around a curling brush and turns on the hair dryer.

I raise my voice over the dryer, "So, it's only been David? And he's never cheated on me?"

She gives me a troubled look, "Uh, I know you're having trouble remembering things since the wreck, but you've never been a damsel in distress waiting to be rescued. That's why I've always enjoyed being around you and I'm certain that's what drew David to you as well. Don't get me wrong, you're not an unfeeling or hard person—you just stand up for yourself and you usually don't allow people to use you like a welcome mat."

I let her words sink in as she goes back to drying my hair. Her description of me seems so foreign. I've always buckled like a belt under pressure and criticism from my parents to my co-workers to Landon.

"Jess, what about my parents? Are they—living?"

"Yeah, they're still around. You've distanced yourself from them more these last few months though."

What? I love my parents, even if they are super critical of everything I do. "Why?"

"Hmm… that's really the only area of your life that you seem afraid to rock the boat. There were definitely times where they crossed the line and you kept quiet, but you are an only child and afraid of losing them—so I get it. David confronted them though, and you seemed to be doing better with some space."

I look up at her as she switches the hair dryer off and reaches for her straightening iron. 'Wait, David confronted them? —about what?"

"Well, you've had some trouble with anxiety recently," I love how she's sugarcoating it and I stop her to let her know that this isn't news to me before she continues, "Well, your parents were not really supportive about the way you were trying to work through it and they were on your case about it. David, knowing you wouldn't say anything to upset them, laid down some ground rules. They actually respected him and have stayed out of your business. And they know that if you want any of their opinions on your mental health, you'll come to them—not vice versa."

I'm positively beaming, "He sounds almost too perfect. Please tell me he has some flaw!"

Jess chuckles at this and sprays my hair into place before picking up the tube of concealer and going to work on my face. She's gently dabbing the make-up around my bruises and stitches when she answers.

"You fight—just like any married couple. You argue about money from time to time. Nobody's perfect. Now close your eyes and let me do your eye shadow." It seems she considers that the final answer on the matter.

When she finishes my make-up, she helps me up to change into the pajamas before getting me settled back into bed. She finds a pocket mirror in her purse and shows me her handiwork. She's done an amazing job of masking my bruises and cuts—they seem a lot less noticeable now. I still have this nagging feeling that things aren't quite as they seem. "I have to be honest, Jess. This doesn't feel real. It's like some alternate universe where I get my happily ever after. That doesn't happen in real life."

"I know this has got to be so strange for you, Lizzie. I can't imagine waking up and everything being different. Just know that you're surrounded by people who love you and I'm always here if you need to talk."

"Jess, I love you. Thank you so much for doing this." She leans her forehead lightly against mine, "What kind of friend would I be if I left this task up to your 'new' husband?" We both laugh at the thought of David wielding a mascara wand.

CHAPTER FIFTEEN

David comes in a little while later to find us both sitting in bed, laughing together. "Beth, you seem to be doing well," He stops suddenly as he takes me in, "My God, you look— just amazing. I'm speechless."

I feel like I'm having a hot flash. Jess's mouth drops open, "David, I'll take that as a nod to my skills. You're welcome." Her words are dripping with sarcasm and David appears to tense up.

He glances over at her, "No, my wife looks good even without all the makeup," before coming over to me. "You know that, right? Are you sure you're not faking this whole head injury thing?" I scrunch my nose as he places a kiss on it and then settles into the chair. Jess leaves soon after, promising to stop by the next day, just as Dr. Briggs comes into the room.

"I've got some good news, Elizabeth. I've got the results from the tests we ran earlier and they show normal brain function. Now, that's not to say you don't have a brain injury—it just means that there is no visible damage or swelling of the brain. This confirms our earlier tests as well. With the exception of remembering your husband, you are aware of surroundings. I would feel confident in releasing you tomorrow morning if you continue to show improvement. However, I do recommend getting you in with a rehab facility to see if we can regain the part of your memory lost to you."

David interjects, "Dr. Briggs, Beth has been seeing a therapist as well. Do you think it might help for her to make an appointment there?"

"In addition to seeing a neuropsychologist—it certainly wouldn't hurt. I'll make my rounds around seven tomorrow morning and if things remain the same, we'll get you discharged and make a follow up appointment for therapy."

This is good news right? I get to go home and live my life with David—just the two of us—all alone. What happens if I can't remember anything though? I cannot go there right now. I've already had one panic attack today—*deep breaths, in and out.* I look over at David, "—So, I'm still seeing Dr. White once a month? Is my anxiety well-managed normally?"

He exhales slowly, "Well, you haven't been seeing her that long and if you asked me a while back, I'd say you were the last person to need therapy. In the last year though, you've had an attack three to four times a month. I don't know if it's because we've been trying to get pregnant and it hasn't happened yet, but you've been on edge. You've just been under tremendous amounts of stress with that, your job, and me traveling for work."

"Wait—you travel for work? Aren't you a construction worker?" I'm puzzled and I realize belatedly that I have no idea if construction workers travel outside of the city they live in. In fact, I know next to nothing about construction.

He looks bemused, "Well, technically I own the company, but I've been running almost all aspects of the business trying to get us off the ground so I guess you could call me a 'construction worker' and as for the travel—I try to stay in town. The past year has brought a lot of out-of-town work though. I want to be close to you, but we were offered a pretty big job up north that would not only bring a lot of money, but recognition for the company as well. It's a three to four month job and I planned on turning it down until you went and changed my mind." He squeezes in next to me in the bed.

"So, you're out of town how often?" I can feel my heart rate picking up in my chest. I had no idea what Landon, the man I saw every day was up to, how am I supposed to keep tabs on a husband who spends the majority of his time in a different city?

"I usually leave Sunday nights and come home early Friday evenings. Obviously, I'm going to stay with you until you're back to feeling like yourself again—Hey, don't cry. C'mere." He pulls me to his chest and strokes his hand up and down my back, "I promise I'm staying until you're ready for me to get out of your hair."

I press myself into him, breathing him in. He smells of leather and soap. *He loves me. He loves me and he would never do anything to hurt me. He is a good man.* I repeat the mantra in my head over and over again until I feel myself relaxing and sleep beckoning once again.

There's country music blasting through my SUV's speakers. It sounds like George, or Kenny, or who am I kidding? I prefer Broadway to Nashville so I have no idea. I roll my eyes at David as he turns it up louder. "Really? Is this necessary right now?" I have to raise my voice to be heard. I hear the horns and glance to my right. Someone's run the light. Was it us? I can hear the brakes from other cars squeal as they lock down, the acrid smell of burning rubber from the tires hangs heavy in the air. The smell turns my stomach. I cannot understand why the other drivers are braking and then everything goes dark.

I jolt awake, my heart pounding in my chest, "David!" He comes out of the bathroom and is by my side in seconds.

'What's wrong? Are you hurting?"

93

"I-I-I dreamed about the wreck. I'm sorry; I'm just so shaken up right now. It's like it just happened." Even my voice is unsteady.

He strokes the hair back off of my forehead, "Shhhh, you're safe here. Do you remember any specifics?"

"Yeah, we were listening to country music and you turned it up even louder because I rolled my eyes. And then there were horns honking because someone ran the light. Is any of that even remotely accurate?"

David is nodding, "You're remembering. That's my girl. Although I'm still holding out hope that country music will grow on you," seeing my incredulous look he laughs, "Hey, miracles can happen!"

I smile at him, but I'm still struggling to make sense of my dream. The song I heard in the accident was the same one playing in the bar the night I went out with Jess and I thought the exact same thing both times.

CHAPTER SIXTEEN

"David, how did we meet?" He's gone and smuggled in real food for dinner—hamburgers—and we're just about to dig in when the question finds its way out of my mouth.

"We met at a bar one night. You dumped your drink all over me after getting your heel caught in the deck on the patio."

"Malibu and pineapple, right?" Thank God, I actually remember the details as they happened, granted they occurred last night for me and not four years ago.

"Yes ma'am, you kept saying I smelled delicious—like candy," He grins at me. "I got your number at the end of the night and I couldn't even wait a full day before I called you. We've talked every day since."

"So, I didn't mix anxiety medication and alcohol and then fall and hit my head?"

David's smile fades and he looks perplexed, "No, you had two drinks—three if I count the one you dumped on me. I mean, it's been awhile, but as I remember it—you seemed fine that night."

We eat in silence, both of us trying to understand where the other is coming from. I'm baffled—I can remember the majority of the details of our first meeting, but I cannot even begin to fathom how my mind created an alternate ending. Wait a minute—"David, was Jess with me that night? Her and oh, what was his name—tattoo boy?"

He has just taken a sip of his drink and chokes with laughter at my question. "Tattoo boy? You mean Nate? Yeah, they were both there. I seem to recall you feeling like a third wheel that night."

Whoa. Tattoo boy has a name?

"Did they get married?"

"Yeah, they got married." He is obviously not going to elaborate.

This is nothing like I remember. Jess has always been the crazy, irresponsible one. And, why wouldn't she have mentioned her family when she was here earlier? I even teased her about leaving me to go out on a hot date when she left earlier—*oh no. I am the worst friend.* I'm sure she thought I was mental, but thankfully she kept it to herself. "I never saw Jess as monogamous. That means she's probably not taking a different guy home every night either then." I clap my hand over my mouth. *That was my outside voice! What is it about being in front of David that makes every stray thought come flying out of my mouth?*

He's definitely taken aback and what? Disappointed? His voice is eerily calm though, "I can't say how Jess used to be— I know you've said she could get pretty wild back in the day. I—"

I interrupt him, "I'm sorry. That was an incredibly rude thing to say. I just have so many jumbled images in my head of how people are and I can't make heads or tails from it yet. It's like a puzzle I'm trying to piece back together in my mind."

He cups my cheek with his hand, "I know. It's going to be rough for a while. Your memory will come back though; I just can't allow myself to think anything else."

I agree before blurting out, "You're the reason my parents haven't come by yet, aren't you?"

David stands up abruptly and begins gathering up the trash from our meal before throwing it away (with a bit more force than was required). "Yeah, I guess I'm the bad guy now. I just wanted you to be as relaxed as possible and you can't get that when your mom's here. She's so negative about everything you do."

"Thank you. Really, I mean it. She's hard to deal with under normal circumstances—at least the way I remember it. You did the right thing."

He visibly relaxes and comes back over to me. "I'm sorry, Beth. This whole thing has me on edge. I alternate between being so thankful that you're alive to feeling completely frustrated that you can't remember our life together. I need to remember that I promised you 'for better or for worse' and maybe down a couple of beers in the meantime."

I reach over and stroke his hand, "I can think of something we could do to relax you," seeing him cock an eyebrow and glance over at the hospital room door I hastily amend my statement. "I mean we could kiss—you know, keep it rated PG in case a nurse walks in." *Keep it rated PG?* Oh, if I could bury my face under the covers in shame. My inner romantic is wincing at my failed attempt at seduction, and picks up her copy of *Fifty Shades of Grey* instead. Ouch!

David just grins at me, clearly entertained by my ineptitude, "It's good to see that you've retained your awkwardness when it comes to all things intimate."

Before I can voice a rebuttal, he leans in, placing his mouth over mine and any argument I had is quickly forgotten. He kisses me like he's never going to get another chance to, there's just so much passion there. And even though we're sitting in a hospital room, this feels like home.

CHAPTER SEVENTEEN

Dr. Briggs discharges me exactly as promised the next morning. David gathers up the various flower arrangements and plants from around the room along with the duffel bag Jess brought before heading down to get his truck. Even Kassie drops in to see me off, "I hope you just continue to improve every day." I hug her and promise that I will before two male volunteers come in with a wheelchair to take me downstairs.

Thank goodness David grabbed me some spare clothes when he ran home or I'd be parading around in the pajamas Jess brought. The anxious feelings thrust their way into my consciousness and I have to talk myself down. *I'm going home. I don't know where home is, but I'm going there. Everything is good. Just breathe—in and out.* It doesn't seem to be working as well as I'd hoped when I look up and see David pull under the blue awning of the pick-up zone in a dark gray Ford F-250 Crew Cab. *That's got to be a fifty thousand dollar vehicle—at least!* He jumps down from the driver side and comes over to me and my mouth goes dry. *That, ladies and gentlemen, is the cure for anxiety.*

"You ready to go home, Beth?"

I nod, still speechless from the image of him in that truck. I never thought of myself as a truck person before the accident, but lord help me—he just became even sexier. He helps me out of the wheelchair and then picks me up and puts me in the truck. He does it like a man carries his new bride over the threshold and the symbolism is not lost on me.

We drive home in relative silence, my hand in his. When we pull up to our garage I'm taken aback. It's the same house as before—the very same house that Landon and I lived in. David looks over at me to see if there's any spark of recognition and breaks into a big grin when he sees the look on my face. "I remember this place," I note the empty garage, "but where's my car?"

"Your car is totaled, remember? I haven't had time to deal with any of that stuff yet. First thing tomorrow though, we'll call the insurance company and find out what's being done—see if we can't get you something else to drive before I go back to work." I think to myself that he'd make a great parent. He's already so patient with a wife who has the memory of a goldfish.

I expect to walk into the house and find it exactly like I remembered it from before. While the layout is the same, the décor's completely inconsistent with my memories. Before, everything was pristine with neutral colors. It looked like a home you'd see in a design magazine.

Where it seemed a bit cold before, lacking in personal touches; my fingerprints are now all over the place. Gone is the leather furniture in the living room—the walls are a light shade of blue that reminds me of the beach, the side furniture is hand painted, and there are canvases with bold pops of color on them. It's as if I hit up the flea market every weekend to design this room—I love it.

"How did I find all of this stuff?"

David yawns and stretches his arms over his head (the hospital cot was obviously not good to him) before sinking down onto the couch, "Well, you refinished all the furniture yourself. We went to garage and estate sales to find the materials. The canvases are yours too."

I'm shocked. *I can paint?* "I did this? I didn't even know I was capable of anything like that. It's fantastic." I'm running my hands along the side tables, trying to take it all in. There are pictures of us all along the mantle and adjoining bookshelves. How could I forget this?

He's resting his head against the back of the couch and his eyes are closed, "Yeah, we have a deal. You have free reign on anything to do with the inside of this house, but I hold the rights to all decisions pertaining to the front and back yard."

I chuckle and toss a pillow at his head and he opens one eye to glare at me, "Really, Beth? Can't a guy get some rest?"

Like a dog being thrown a stick, I move towards the bedroom, "Yes, great idea. I can't wait to see what our bedroom looks like!" He groans as he gets up to follow me. Our bedroom is done in a vintage Hollywood style with light stone-colored walls, dark hardwood flooring, a thick white rug you could get lost in, mirrored dressers, a dark gray upholstered headboard on a King-sized bed—there's even an old-fashioned vanity complete with a mirror and cushioned stool. It's perfect. Well, almost— "If only we had an antique chandelier we could hang."

David is sitting on the edge of the bed, removing his shoes. "Beth, we live in Texas. There is no way we're getting rid of a ceiling fan that we use nine months out of the year so that you have something sparkly to look at. Why don't you check out the bathroom though—you might be pleased with the compromise."

I look into the bathroom to find that there's a beautiful chandelier suspended above the deep tub. *My man delivered.*

I want to hug him, I'm so happy. I feel like it's Christmas Day and I just received everything on my list. *Super hot husband who's madly in love with me? Check. A house that's the manifestation of every design fantasy I've had? Double check.* I pad back into the bedroom, ready to thank him, when I hear his deep, even breathing. He looks pretty good even when he's completely exhausted. I kick off my shoes and crawl under the covers next to him.

CHAPTER EIGHTEEN

I dream of a darkened bedroom and warm skin draped over me like a blanket. His lips brush mine and I am on fire. "You taste so good," he sighs against my mouth and his voice alone could send me over the edge. I find my hands roaming over the stubble on his face and up into his shaggy hair, anything to try and anchor myself. He pulls back and looks at me. "Are you sure?" His voice is just above a whisper. We've reached a crossroads here and I find myself in unfamiliar territory. Tonight, he offered me everything by asking me to marry him and in return, I want to give him all of me. With trembling hands and a racing heart, I look into his eyes to answer him, "Yes, I want this—I want you." He brings my jittery hands up and places a kiss on each one. "Trust me?" I nod with a shiver. He reaches over to his nightstand and grabs a foil packet. He asks me again, "Are you sure?" and I bring my mouth up to his in response. Inside I'm quaking, but I need him. What if I'm not any good? What if he thinks he made a mistake? He cups the side of my face with his hand and I focus on his eyes and push the negative thoughts away. My hands press against his shoulders, not sure whether I want to draw him in or push him out as the pain radiates throughout my lower body. He breaks through a barrier and warmth spreads around us. I'm bleeding. Something's wrong. Sensing my unease, he stills, "It's okay, it's normal. Do you want me to stop?" Afraid that my voice no longer works, I shake my head vigorously—no. He enters me further and the pain subsides. My body begins to take over and I now see why people enjoy this. The pleasure begins to build. He never takes his eyes off of mine and I have never felt so safe. He pushes me to the brink and I fall, crying out his name.

"Beth? Beth, wake up," I open my eyes and it takes me a second to get my bearings and remember where I am. David's hands are on my arms, a troubled look on his face, "Are you okay? You were moaning in your sleep, I thought you might be hurting." I'm certain my face just became a lovely shade of crimson and I force my eyes closed from the sheer embarrassment of it all. *I have to say something.* "I had a nightmare." *Yes, very good. Nice save.* I open my eyes to gauge his reaction and find him grinning wolfishly down at me. *Yeah, he's not buying that.*

"You had a nightmare, huh? Because, I gotta be honest with you—you're wearing your 'I just had a sex dream' face. Come to think of it, those didn't really sound like moans of pain either." I bite my lower lip in frustration and manage to sit up, crossing my arms across my chest in an attempt to subdue my nipples.

"Yes, it was a very frightening-um-nightmare. Thank you for waking me up." *Throw an "um" in there and he'll totally buy it now.* My inner romantic is fanning herself to cool down. I need to change the subject and quickly before my body takes over and I decide to re-enact my dream with him. *Think of something off-topic. Like the weather, or sports, or*—"So, I was a virgin when we met?" *Oh God. That's not a different topic at all.* My inner romantic tosses the fan down and sits up eagerly.

Now, it's David's turn to look shocked. Obviously, he didn't see the conversation going here. He opens and closes his mouth several times, choosing his words no doubt. "Yeah—wait. That's what you dreamed about—the night I asked you to marry me? It is isn't it?" I nod at him and he runs his tongue across his teeth, "Oh Beth that was an amazing night. You were just..." His voice trails off as he meanders down memory lane. He lightly runs his fingers up the inside of my thigh. My stomach growls and he snaps back to reality. "We'll come back to this later, but first—let's get you some dinner."

I'm looking through the fridge trying to find something to cook up for us. Saturday is my grocery day, *I think,* and seeing as to how I was in the hospital then, the shelves are just about empty. I scrounge up a bag of salad greens and a tomato.

"David? I think we may need to order in tonight. Unless a salad will fill you up?"

He stops rummaging through the pantry, "I don't think so. I'll run out and get us something. Jess is on her way over to see you," He runs his hand through his hair, "Anything you're hungry for?"

Just you—no, you cannot say that. I compose my thoughts, "Maybe pizza?" *Good girl.*

"I'll swing by *West Crust.* Sound good?"

I smile, "I love their pizza?" *I'm assuming so or he wouldn't have suggested it.*

He walks over and kisses me, "I'll be back soon. Jess should be here any moment." I wrap my arms around his waist and slide my hands into the back pocket of his jeans, pulling him in closer to me. The man is leaving me breathless.

"Maybe once she's gone, we can get back to our discussion." *That was brazen*—I'm just as surprised by what's coming out of my mouth as he is.

He taps his index finger against my lips, "Have I told you how lucky I am?" before heading out to the garage.

I decide to explore my house some more while I wait for Jess to arrive. I walk over to the fireplace and stare at our wedding picture. We're standing outside. I'm wearing a gorgeous pearl tea-length gown and my hair is side-swept into loose curls. David is wearing a white dress shirt and cream-colored linen pants. It's so simple and informal. *If only I could remember it.*

There are two guest bedrooms down the hall and I make my way into them. The first one holds a wrought iron bed and more painted furniture. It's very shabby chic. The second room is empty—*this must be the nursery.* My heart tightens a little as I look around. *Why can't I get pregnant?* I've never had any complications or issues during my yearly exams—I mean as far as I can remember. It's a mystery. However, the doorbell prevents me from dwelling on it further.

I open the front door to find Jess holding a small bag. "I've brought my stuff to clean up that shaggy mess your husband calls hair. Where's David?" She tosses the words over her shoulder to me as she comes inside and sets down all her stuff on the dining room table.

"He went to grab some food for dinner."

"Well, the minute he gets back, I'm trimming that hair."

"I kind of like it longer. I think he should leave it." Jess purses her lips as though she is going to argue, but decides against it and sits down on the sofa

I sit down opposite her, "Did you know we'd been trying to have a baby?" *I give up. Every stray thought is going to force its way out of my mouth it seems.*

Jess nods sadly.

"Are David and I seeing a fertility specialist or anything like that?"

"Well, most specialists won't see you until you've been trying for over a year, so no."

I don't say anything. *Time for a topic change*—"Jess, can you grab my phone?" My head is starting to hurt again.

"I'm pretty sure your phone was destroyed in the car wreck."

Of course it was. Everything I thought I knew about my life was destroyed in that car wreck, what's a cell phone compared to that?

We sit in silence together, neither of us knowing quite what to say to the other when David gets back with the pizza. He smiles when he sees me and walks over to the couch, "You feeling okay, babe? Up for some pizza?"

I smile and nod at him, feeling every bit the awkward teenager.

I can't keep the smile off my face when I notice Jess studying me. When she realizes I'm watching her, she looks away. "David, you ready to get rid of that shaggy mess?" *That's weird. It was like she was gauging my reaction to him.*

He looks over at her for the first time since he walked in, "Nah, Jess. I'm thinking of keeping it this length. And I don't wanna rush you, but I'd really love to have a quiet dinner with my wife—" At that, the doorbell rings again. *Are we always this popular?*

David walks over and opens the door to—*Mike?* I feel as though I might be sick. He greets David with a hug. "I was in the neighborhood and thought I'd drop by and check on the patient. How are you holding up, man?"

"I'm fine. That hospital cot was a bitch though. As for Beth, I'll let you see for yourself." He gestures over to me and Mike gives Jess a head tip before coming to stand before me.

"You look good, Elizabeth. How are you feeling?" I can feel my heart racing in my chest. I have so many questions for the man in front of me. If he's not Landon's best friend, then he's— "Are you and David close?"

He shoots a look of confusion over my shoulder at David. Jess cuts in, "Mike, Lizzie cannot remember much of her life before the wreck. She didn't even know who David was."

Mike looks stricken by the revelation. "What the fuck, man? You said she was banged up, you failed to mention amnesia. Is it permanent?"

"You know I'm sitting right here. You could just ask me," I laugh as I say it even though my every nerve is strung as tight as a bow string.

"Mike, let's talk on the patio and give the ladies a few minutes to catch up before dinner. I'll meet you outside, let me just get my beautiful wife a drink first." He goes over to the bar area where there's a wine refrigerator sitting on the counter. *Oh, how did I miss that before? More wine? Wait, that's not wine—it's champagne!* "You know that champagne is my favorite?"

Jess looks up from her phone and snorts with laughter, "Lizzie, everyone knows that champagne is your favorite."

David pauses in opening the bottle and lowers his voice, "Of course. I also know that it is absolutely not because it feels like a tickle when the bubbles touch your lips."

He laughs at my open-mouthed expression. *So much for keeping that tidbit to myself—* "That was supposed to be a secret."

He pours me a glass and brings it over to me. "I promise not to tell a soul," he whispers and kisses me on the nose before going outside to meet Mike.

Jess remains deep in thought over something on her phone. I sit back down on the couch with my champagne and wait for her to finish. She and I need to talk.

CHAPTER NINETEEN

I decide to take the bull by the horns while my husband is preoccupied, "Jess, why were you staring at me earlier? You looked pretty intense."

She looks down at her phone again, avoiding eye contact with me. "I don't know, Lizzie. You just seemed so happy and relaxed, but also—vulnerable. I just don't remember the last time I saw you like that—you usually seemed stressed out over something; this accident just seems to have made you different—in a good way."

—*Vulnerable? If only she could've seen me in my imaginary past life?* "I'm sorry. I didn't want it to sound like I was trying to come down on you, but I just felt like you were judging me. I wanted to clear the air so that I don't replay it over and over in my head later."

She scoots over next to me and takes my hand, "We were so worried after the wreck when you wouldn't wake up and now I guess I'm still expecting to catch glimpses of the old you in there. Please know that I would never judge you. You are such a good person, Lizzie." I dab at my eyes with my fingers. She really is like the sister I never had. She leaves soon after, insisting she has dinner plans.

I'm sitting on the couch, working through my second glass of champagne and a slice of pizza while watching the neighborhood kids revel in the last hour of daylight when David comes back in alone.

"Where's Mike?"

He grabs a slice of pizza and comes over to me, "He got called in to work a shift tonight, so he had to run."

"What is it that he does exactly?"

David laughs, "I'm an idiot. Of course you don't know what he does. He's a cop, Beth. Do you remember him, from before?"

"A little," I swallow hard, "Isn't he uh married to Katie?" My palms are sweating as I wait for him to respond.

He looks at me as though I've grown two heads, "Mike, married? Jesus, Beth, you really don't remember him at all do you?"

My cheeks burn and I feel like a moron. David leans over and grabs my hand, his voice soft, "Hey, I didn't mean to make you feel bad. I get it, I do—you've got a lot of questions. It's just that the idea of Mike remaining with one woman long enough to marry her is almost impossible to imagine." He laughs again and I swear, I could listen to that sound all day.

Seeing that I'm content, he leaves me to take a shower and "wash off the hospital." I'm just psyching myself up to join him when he walks back in wearing a pair of black athletic shorts and nothing else, his hair damp. He grabs another slice of pizza and a beer from the fridge before coming back over to me. *Do not stare at his well-sculpted chest. Do not stare at his tattoos. Keep your cool. He is not a piece of meat...a delicious cut of prime rib...Fuck.*

"Beth, you want some more pizza? You're staring at it like you're starving."

"Uh, no thank you. I'm good—just zoned out," *Nice save.* I'm mentally high-fiving myself when I notice something. "Is that my name across your ribs?"

He pauses mid-bite and glances down to where my name is engraved on the left side of his chest, starting at the base of his ribs and curving upward, "Yeah, I got it when we got married. I had it done across my ribs because of a passage I like in the Bible— 'This one is bone from my bone and flesh from my flesh! She will be called woman, because she was taken from man.' It's from Genesis 2:23 when Eve is created for Adam."

I blink quickly to dispel the tears—I'm touched. In this moment, I realize just how much I love this man and how much he loves me. On the other hand, he now looks like he wants to crawl under a rock. "David, I'm blown away. That's the most beautiful thing anyone has ever done for me." There's no blinking away these tears and it quickly becomes full-on weeping. *This is all stress from the accident. It's completely normal.* I just feel so undeserving of all of this.

He sets the beer and pizza down and pulls me to my feet. "You know, you loved the tattoo when I got it, but showing it to you again—I was a little nervous. They say head injuries can do weird things to a person; stuff that you loved before, you hate, and vice-versa. It's a lot of pressure for a man!" He laughs and I lean against him, smiling.

Suddenly serious, he tilts my chin up, "I love you— more than anything in this world and I would give my life protecting you. I need you to know that." He wipes my tears away with his thumb and kisses me.

"I love you too, David. Part of me feels like I just met you two days ago, but there's another part that feels like it's been us—you and me— forever," He leans down to kiss me again and I stop him, "Can I just take a minute, please? I just want to shower and compose myself."

He agrees and I go into the bathroom, locking the door behind me. *What if this isn't real? What if I'm still lying on the patio at Nick's? Maybe this is like that movie The Family Man and I'm having a glimpse of what my life could be like with David.*

My head is starting to hurt again. If it's just a glimpse, that doesn't explain the memories of life with him coming back though. I also don't know how to explain how I have memories of a life with a man who doesn't exist either. You know what? I don't care what the explanation is. I have a man in that living room that loves me and makes me feel alive. I take a deep breath to steady myself and glance over at the tub. *A bubble bath is much more appealing than a shower. I need to scrub the hospital off of my skin and it'll buy me a little more time to relax and clear my mind.*

While the water runs, I pick up an iPod from its docking station on the bathroom counter. *Let's see what we've got to work with here. How many country songs can one man listen to? Aren't there any play-lists? Ooh, "Beth's wind-down music"—that looks promising. Don't mind if I do.*

I ease into the deep tub of steamy water and mountains of bubbles and sigh happily. David's always getting on to me for running the water so hot, "If your skin turns dark red, the water is way too hot." I'm constantly reminding him that I want to ensure the germs I've picked up throughout the day die a fiery death.

I jolt. *Wow. I just regained a memory, while still conscious.* Surely, that's a sign of progress. John Mayer is crooning softly about the edge of desire and I slip under the water with a smile on my face.

I pull myself reluctantly from the warm water sometime later to see that it is fully dark outside. I wrap a towel around me and step into my closet. I feel something prick the back of my mind, but no matter how much I try to focus, I can't decipher what it is I'm supposed to remember.

Ellie Goulding's wailing pulls me back to the present and I smile to myself. *Anything could happen. Tonight, I'm going to test that theory.* I find myself moving to the beat of the music and singing along as I sift through the wooden drawers, stopping only when my sore ribs protest.

I stand in front of the bathroom mirror, evaluating my choice in lingerie. The ivory slip has a lace halter top and a satin body with more lace at the hemline. *He certainly won't misinterpret your intentions in this. Maybe I should just stick with a baggy t-shirt and a pair of shorts.* My inner romantic gives my current choice a thumbs up. I quash my doubts and pull my hair out of a bun, letting the loose curls run wild. After checking my reflection for the umpteenth time (I still look pretty rough with the cuts and bruises down the side of my face), I take my glasses off and leave them by the sink before switching off the music and lights and going back into the bedroom.

I can hear the television going in the living room. *He's sprawled out across the couch catching up on the sports world while simultaneously checking his work emails.* I'm startled by the thought. It would be nice if my brain would just release all the memories at once and not little trickles of information at unexpected moments such as this.

I turn the ceiling fan light off and dim the recessed lighting. I want us to be able to see each other, but I certainly don't want to feel like I'm under a spotlight. After wrestling with the pillow placement for several minutes, I toss them all to the floor in frustration. I need this to be perfect and the universe is conspiring against me. I go over and pick up each pillow, placing them on the upholstered bench at the foot of the bed.

It takes a few more tries before I feel that room is ready for romance. There are only two pillows on the bed—*a nice compromise*, and the covers are gently turned back. *Now, do I lie across the bed seductively or stand next to it mysteriously?* I throw my hands up in defeat.

"Uh, David? Could you come here?"

CHAPTER TWENTY

"Sure Beth, you okay?"— the words die on his lips as he takes in the scene in front of him; the dim lights and me perched halfway on the bed in what I thought was a seductive, but now realize comes across as a stiff pose. He looks amused, "You comfortable sitting like that?" My inner romantic has tipped back in her chair, laughing hysterically. A lot of help she is.

"No, not really, I feel like an amateur at this kind of stuff."

His grin widens, "And what kind of 'stuff' are you referring to?"

Disaster. Abort! Abort! This was a terrible idea. "I just thought—it's stupid really. I'll change." I need the earth to swallow me up.

He's over to me in just a few strides, "Stop. It's perfect. I didn't want to push you until you felt comfortable. I mean, you just met me two nights ago. Don't you think it's a little soon for you to be taking me to bed?" I swat him on the arm and he smirks at me.

"You're teasing me; after all the effort I just went to. Hmm…maybe we should wait," He leans me back against the mattress and stops me with his mouth. I pull away, "Are you sure you don't want me to sleep in the guest room?"

"Don't you fucking dare. There's no way in hell I'm letting you walk out of this room." He practically growls the words and I find myself shivering in anticipation. "Did you intentionally wear your wedding night lingerie, Beth?"

"What? No, I didn't remember—it's kind of fitting though don't you think?" I bring his mouth back to mine and use my hands to guide him onto his back.

I feel much more in control as I sit on top of him. The athletic shorts cannot hide his erection. The fact that I've turned him on only ignites the fire within me. His hands keep finding the hem of my slip and trying to work it up, but I shake my head "no". This is about remembering. I want to savor every moment and see if I can't unlock a few more memories in the process. I run my fingers lightly across the stubble on his chin before turning his head and taking his ear lobe between my teeth. He groans and his hands are clawing at my back, searching. I work my way down and place a kiss across his ribs and my name, with him fruitlessly trying to arch up into me, his hands fisting my hair. I'm feeling pretty proud of my sexual prowess when he sits up suddenly and pushes me back into the pillows before stripping off his athletic shorts. *Oh. My. God. He is very happy to have me home. Stop staring! Mazel tov to me.* I bite down on the tip of my index finger and look up into his eyes. *Yeah bite your finger, good idea—that calmed him down.*

He climbs back onto the bed and grips the hem of my slip. He murmurs, "Someone's wearing too many clothes," before pulling it up and over my head and then it's his turn to drink me in with his eyes—*and his mouth. Oh sweet lord, his mouth.* He uses his thumb and index finger to tease my nipples before taking one in his mouth. I feel slight panic setting in with the thought that I'm cheating. *Stop. This is your husband. He is the only man you've ever been with and the only one you will ever be with. He loves you. This is right.* The thought calms me immensely. He's pushing me to a fever pitch. I pull him back up to my mouth, breathlessly exclaiming, "I want you so badly," before my body fractures against his hand.

David pulls away and reaches over to his nightstand and I surprise myself, "Stop, we don't need it."

He looks over his shoulder, "Are you sure? We don't have to try tonight."

"I want to do this and I really want to feel you inside of me. Nothing else…please."

He mutters a curse before shoving the top drawer closed and making his way back to me, "God, do you have any idea what it does to me when you talk like that?"

Before I can form an articulate response, he's inside of me and all I can do is moan his name over and over as an intense orgasm washes over me. He pulls me over to the side of the bed and I come again, almost instantly. David is like a man possessed, there is no soft and sweet here. It's as if he's trying to fuck me into remembering my life with him. His thrusting increases and I can no longer tell where one orgasm begins and the other ends. He groans my name as he comes and tears of happiness streak down my face. He holds my head in his hands as he kisses the tears away.

We fall asleep wrapped around each other in a tangle of limbs. My inner romantic lights a cigarette as she lounges on her chaise. He pulls me to him twice in the middle of the night, as if needing to reassure himself that I'm real. I worry that it won't be as good as the first time and he proves me wrong each time. He's gentler with me and I find that I can't decide which I like better with him: soft and sweet or rough. I think, *maybe I'm dead. That would explain why this feels like heaven.*

CHAPTER TWENTY-ONE

I wake up to the sound of the shower and look over at the clock. It takes a second for my eyes to adjust enough to make it out—nine-thirty? I don't remember the last time I slept in that late. I smile remembering why I was up half the night and tiptoe into the bathroom to see if David needs help getting clean.

He doesn't even seem surprised to see me standing there. He opens the door and pulls me into him, under a cascade of warm water. *We've been together for four years, but it all feels so new to me. Maybe all it takes is a head injury to spice up your marriage.* He takes the soap and lathers it generously across my breasts and belly, taking great care to ensure I'm clean. When he tilts my head back and trails kisses down my neck and across my collarbone, I shiver even with the warm water running down my body. He gently picks me up and uses the wall as a brace before entering me. My sore muscles protest initially, but the pain is forgotten within seconds. We come at the same time, wrapped up in each other. While the majority of me is enjoying the moment, there's still a small part of my brain that is waiting for something to click. I feel as though my memories are just out of reach.

I'm sitting at the café table on our back patio, cup of coffee in hand. I take a small sip before leaning back in my chair and taking in the day. Summer has always been my favorite. We've made it past the spring dirt-storms and now there's nothing but clear blue skies overhead. There's a flower bed along the fence bursting with red and orange blanket flowers and black-eyed Susan plants. Several bees flit from flower to flower, their hum soothing. A small water feature bubbles in the corner of the yard and a few birds land to take a drink. "You look so damn adorable sitting there staring off into space." David's voice startles me out of my thoughts and I turn to him, smiling.

"You look pretty good yourself, Mr. Greene." He comes over and sits down in the other chair with his coffee.

He gestures to his cell phone, "Sorry about the back-to-back phone calls—gotta put out some fires. It's the downside to being my own boss."

I give him a mischievous smile, "I had plenty to keep my mind occupied."

"Is that so? You'll have to enlighten me later," he runs his fingers through the stubble on his face and grins, "First things first though. We're going to get you a new phone and grab some lunch before you go see Dr. White at one-thirty."

"You got me in? Thank you."

"That was one of the phone calls I made just before dealing with work. I thought it might help to see another familiar face and she might be able to help you piece this together."

I go over and sit down on his lap, "You really are the best."

He runs a finger across my collar-bone and says huskily, "Now, let's discuss these thoughts you were having while I was on the phone."

Replacing my phone turns out to be easier than expected as I was due for an upgrade. The sales agent asks me if I have an online storage account and we're able to retrieve all of my contacts and photos. My phone begins chirping soon afterward as text messages and voicemails pour in. There are quite a few texts from Lauren. I turn to David, "You let my work know I was out right?"

His face is a mask of confusion, "Yeah, why?"

I show him my phone, "Lauren's been texting me."

He shrugs, "She's probably just checking in on you. She knows you're out indefinitely though. In fact, she was going to stop by and bring dinner one night this week."

Now it's my turn to look confused, "Did she come by to see me when I was in the hospital?"

"Beth, she was the first one there Friday night. I've never seen her so upset. She's been covering for you at work, so she told me she'd be over the first chance she got." So, she and I are friends in this realm too. That's a comforting thought. I scroll through several of the messages and see that they were sent the day I woke up.

"Are you awake?"   9:56 PM

"Can I come see you?" 11:01 PM

The others are a mix of wondering how I am and what I'm doing. That's sweet of her to reach out like that. *Maybe she's turning over a new leaf as well.* I shoot her a quick reply.

"Doing well. Finally free of the hospital gown ;-) See you soon!"

We grab lunch at a nearby Mexican food restaurant as it's "Taco Tuesday"—*David's favorite.* I grin as another detail falls into place. This puzzle is coming together quite nicely, albeit a little slower than I'd hoped. I spend our lunch together getting to know my husband. "Where are your parents?"

It takes him a second to answer me as he finishes chewing, "My mom lives down in Beaumont, close to the gulf

119

and my dad passed away a year ago from a sudden heart-attack." He tightens his mouth and I reach for his hand.

"I'm so sorry. I wouldn't have brought it up if I could just remember." I bite my lower lip to keep from tearing up.

"Hey, don't do that. You're doing the best you can. I'm not mad," He squeezes my hand before continuing, "You know, my dad loved you. He said you reminded him of young Lucille Ball with your crazy facial expressions and sense of humor." I pucker my lips and widen my eyes at him (my best impression off-hand) and he laughs, "Yeah Beth, just like that."

CHAPTER TWENTY-TWO

We arrive at Dr. White's office with five minutes to spare so we get comfortable on the love seat in the waiting room. I decide to check in with my mother while waiting.

"Hey, just wanted to let you know that I'm out of the hospital. I'm at a doctor's appointment now, but I'll call you later—I love you."

Dr. White steps out of her office. "Hello, Elizabeth. David—we haven't seen you here in a while." He stands up and shakes her hand as she ushers us both into her office. "Hey Beth, I'm going to sit out in the truck and get some work done if that's alright." I nod at him and follow Dr. White into the office.

It looks exactly the same, which means I didn't imagine it. I settle in on the couch as she sits across from me.

"So, it's been a month since we last met and you're sitting here in front of me looking a little worse for the wear. What's going on with you? What's happening in your life right now?" Her voice is so soothing I feel my throat tighten.

I manage to get through the events of the past few days, only stopping to cry once. I'm so used to seeing Dr. White impassive that it takes me a minute to register her shocked facial expression.

She sputters, "So, you remember nothing?"

"Well, I remember meeting David. It just feels like something that happened three days ago instead of four years ago. And I can remember little things here and there. Overall, it's like my brain is withholding information."

Her notebook slides to the floor, unnoticed. "So, you cannot remember what we've been meeting about over the last year?"

"Wait, you mean I haven't been seeing you for the last five years? Just this year?"

She brings her hand up to her mouth, "Elizabeth, you and I have only been seeing each other a short amount of time. You really don't remember any of it?"

I feel like I'm in trouble, "No, I'm sorry, unless we really did meet about Landon having an affair."

She leans forward in her chair, "Landon? You can remember Landon? That's a start."

Wait—what? Did she mean David—Landon's real?

Now it's my turn to play interrogator, "So, just a minute—you know about Landon?"

She stops me, "What do *you* remember about Landon?"

Is this a joke?

I bring my left hand up to my temple. "I'm not sure what's going on here, Dr. White. No one else has known who Landon is and now you're telling me that he's real? I'm completely confused." I pull at the collar of my blouse, feeling hot.

Her soothing voice is back, "Elizabeth, take a deep breath and relax your mind. It's okay to be confused in all of this. David is here now and that is what matters. Let's talk about how you're recovering at home with him."

My mind is racing, trying to make sense of it all. *He's real. Why am I so disappointed to hear that?*

"I'm sorry, Dr. White. I'm not feeling well," she gives me a puzzled look. "I'll pay you for the full hour, but I need to go lie down." I jump up off of the couch and head for the door with my head down, the bile rising up in my throat.

She follows me to the door, "Elizabeth, please stay. Let's try to talk these feelings out."

I shake my head through my tears. *I can't breathe in this room. I need to get outside.* "I'll have David reschedule later. I just need to get home." I brush past her and into the sunshine outside where I take deep breaths.

David is sitting inside his truck having what appears to be a tense conversation. I can't burden him with this, not after everything he's been dealt the last few days. I wait for him to finish his conversation and compose myself before going over to him.

When I open the door and climb in he looks at the clock, "Wasn't that supposed to be an hour?"

I nod, "My head's really hurting so she decided it would be better if we rescheduled for next week." *I am a little white liar.* My inner romantic is searching the liquor cabinet, looking for a bottle of tequila to deal with this new development. He looks distressed, "Let's get you home and in bed. We just did too much for your first day." I pick at my nails on the drive home, trying to work events out in my head. It's futile.

When we get home, I walk in and throw the covers back on the bed before climbing in fully dressed. David tries to follow me, but his phone begins ringing. I can hear him having a heated discussion with someone from his company. "No, I can't damn well get up there to fix this mess. Why? Because my wife isn't well, that's why!" I hear him sigh, "I don't know when I'll be able to leave."

I get out of bed and make my way to him. He looks worried sick right now. I whisper, "David, you have to go up there."

He glances at me, afflicted by my words, "Let me call you back," He hangs up the phone. "Beth, I can't leave you now. You're not even close to being well. If only they weren't threatening to pull the job out from under us right now."

"You cannot lose this job on my account. Please go up there and do whatever it is construction company owners do to save a job. I'll be fine. I can text Lauren and see if she wants to bring dinner by."

He glances at his watch, "If I leave now I should make it up there right before quitting time and maybe I can round up the guys for a meeting. I will try to be home by tomorrow evening at the latest. Do you want to stay with your parents?"

"No, I'm going to have to get used to you working out of town sometimes. This will be good practice for me."

I go over to where he's sitting and wrap my arms around his neck. He kisses me, "What did I do to get so lucky?"

CHAPTER TWENTY-THREE

David leaves me lying in bed satiated. Turns out he had a few extra minutes to spare, and we took advantage of that. I roll over and grab my phone off the nightstand to text Lauren.

"David had to go back to Amarillo earlier than expected. Do you want to come over and keep me company tonight?"

Her response is immediate.

"Absolutely, what time? Want me to bring dinner?"

I giggle as I type my reply.

"Yes! As long as you're not cooking! And, come at 8?"

There's a joke around our office that all of the fast food restaurants are on a first name basis with Lauren. Not that you'd be able to tell, she's so tiny.

"Deal, I'll pick-up something and see you then."

I'm pretty excited to spend some time with her. We don't ever see each other outside of work. Neither one of us is very social so we tend to head straight home to the comfort of our own couches after a day at the office. She's single and doesn't have any kids—well, pre-accident she didn't. Maybe I can pick her brain and see if we can't trigger some more memories.

I still feel like I'm missing something, but instead of trying to decode my appointment with Dr. White, I choose to nap. I place my phone and glasses on the nightstand. My brain needs some rest.

I wake up and realize from the way the light is streaming in through the window that I slept a lot longer than I meant to. The clock reads seven twenty-three. *Holy Cow—I must've needed some recovery time to make up for last night.* I check my phone to find several texts, one from my mom and one from David. I decide to get the bad news out of the way first by reading my mother's text.

"Glad you are okay. Wish you would learn to call and not just text. Hope you're being good to David."

That was better than I expected even though she still managed to get a guilt trip in there. *Great job, Mom!*

I scroll to the next one from David.

"Hey Beth, hope you got some rest after I left. You seemed pretty worn out for some odd reason. I'm missing you like crazy! I'm about to head to dinner with some of the guys and then I'll call you. Still hoping to get this wrapped up tomorrow so I can come home to you. I love you."

Now that is a text message. Sigh. I realize I'm grinning at the phone screen as if he can see me. I type a quick reply back.

"Slept all afternoon, I wonder why I was so tired? I'm about to get a shower and then Lauren is bringing dinner at eight. I miss you too and cannot wait until I hear your voice again. I love you—more! Ha"

I turn the shower on to warm up and look for something to wear. I settle on a powder blue tank top and a pair of black cotton shorts. I go over to the mirror. What little make-up I was wearing is now long gone and I debate on whether or not to reapply. *It's girls' night. Go au natural.*

After I've showered, I dry my hair and work on taming it, eventually giving up and throwing it into a bun. I look ready for an evening in.

I take the iPod with me into the living room and plug it into the docking station. Eddie Vedder begins singing about hearing sirens in that throaty, raspy voice of his. Instead of straightening up the room, I sit and listen to the words, with tears streaming down my face —thank god I didn't apply more makeup. I grab my phone and text David,

"Sitting here listening to Pearl Jam's 'Sirens' and cannot stop thinking of you. Promise me you'll listen to it tonight?"

His response is immediate.

"I have it downloaded to my phone. It's a perfect song for us. I'll listen to it as soon as I leave dinner. Love you—most!"

I smile and stand up to get my house straightened.

At eight o'clock on the dot, the doorbell rings. *She's prompt, as usual.* I dry my hands on a dish towel and go over to let her in. *I hope she brought spaghetti—* my heart drops.

Standing on my front porch is Landon.

I try to keep the panic out of my voice, "What are you doing here, Landon? I'm expecting someone. You can't be here."

He ignores me and walks in closing the door behind him, "I didn't think he was going to leave your side anytime soon. Let me guess, work needed him. And what the hell is going on with your face? Did that motherfucker do that you?" He looks concerned, but his voice is ice cold.

"It's not important—Lauren is coming over and you cannot be here. We're going to have dinner and then David, my husband, is going to be calling me." I try enunciating every word to get my point across.

"Please tell me there's a reason you're acting like this right now. You knew you weren't texting Lauren. It's been our cover for the last year."

My chest is starting to tighten. I can't breathe. No. No. No. This is not happening.

"I don't know why you're here, but I am happily married. Maybe we had something a long time ago, but I love my husband. We're trying to start a family."

He shakes his head and laughs while I shiver involuntarily. "So, you're getting off birth control then?" Seeing my horrified expression he continues. "You want a child, but not with a man who's married to his job. You couldn't let David know that so you got on the pill."

I place my hands on his chest in an attempt to move him out of my house. The minute his back hits the door, I'm assaulted with an image of us in a very similar situation.

CHAPTER TWENTY-FOUR

I was beyond intoxicated and my body was quaking with need. He was at my door within five minutes. Gone were the suit and tie I'd seen him in when we met, he now stood before me in a fitted gray t-shirt and jeans. His dimples were on full display even through his beard, he was grinning so widely.

He took in my flushed cheeks and disheveled appearance, "Hey, you alright there, Elizabeth?"

I took him by the hand and pulled him into the house, quickly shutting the door behind me. "I'm better than alright...now that you're here."

He was clearly confused, but as I pressed myself into him and up against the door I could tell that there was at least one part of him that knew exactly what I wanted.

He let out a frustrated sigh, "Fuck, Elizabeth, you're married. We can't—" I cut him off by reaching up and taking his bottom lip into my mouth, gently biting down.

A low growl escaped the back of his throat and he lifted me up, grinding me up against him. I broke free to whisper in his ear, "Bedroom. Now."

I pulled my shirt off and tossed it aside as he laid me back on the bed. I sat up and began pulling his shirt free from his jeans and up over his head. The man worked out, it was obvious. Abercrombie models would be jealous of his chiseled chest and well-defined ab muscles. I ran my hands over him, my hands shaking as I worked on unbuttoning his jeans. His hands reached down to cover mine, effectively stopping me.

129

He let out a slow breath, "Slow down. Let's talk for a minute. What's going on here?"

I put on my best seductive pout and try to free my hands. "I'd rather not talk right now," my words sound slurred, even to me, "I want you inside of me."

Instead of pouncing on me, he steps back and runs his hands through his hair—his breathing ragged at this point. "God, you're killing me right now. You know we can't do this though. You're married."

Waves of nausea hit me, "Fuck him. He's never here. He was supposed to come home for the weekend and he cancelled on me...again," I whisper the words. I keep my eyes focused on the design of the comforter, unable to meet his gaze.

"That explains why you're drunk right now, and I want you, but not like this. Hell, you're not thinking straight."

My cheeks burning with embarrassment, I manage to stand up and push past him into the bathroom where I begin splashing cold water onto my face. It's not working. The nausea is only getting worse. Landon walks in just in time to see me vomit copious amounts of vodka into the toilet.

My stomach finally ends its revolt and I lay my face on the toilet seat, exhausted. I'm expecting him to walk out any second when I feel a cold washcloth against my neck. He sinks down to the cold tile floor next to me and rubs my back. I squeeze my eyes shut, trying to stop the flow of tears, but it's no use. I think of David and I feel the urge to vomit again. The tears increase into full-blown sobbing, but he doesn't leave me.

I cry until there is nothing left within me and then he hands me my shirt and helps me to bed.

I sink down to the floor on my knees. "Oh my God—I think I'm having a heart attack. I can't breathe! I can't breathe!" My breath is coming in short little gasps and I'm shaking uncontrollably. I am certain this is what dying feels like.

He sinks down next to me on the floor and takes my hands, "Calm down. You really didn't know? You don't remember?"

I try to taking deep breaths, but it's not working and now I'm sweating. I try to explain as best I can, my teeth chattering, "I-hit-my-head. There was a c-c-car wreck a-a-and I c-c-couldn't remember..." He stops me from elaborating by pulling me close to him. I want to pull away, but I feel so weak right now.

He cradles my head in his hands, "Elizabeth, you're telling me you have amnesia?" He looks even scarier now that he's serious.

My head is starting to swim, "Brain injury—married to you—just met David. I can't—catch—my breath." Landon is shaking me by the shoulders and asking me where my anxiety medication is, but it sounds like he's a million miles away and it's too hard to talk. *Can't he see I'm dying? Why won't he leave me alone?*

He stands up and goes into my bedroom to search for pills and I want to yell that he doesn't belong in there, but it would require too much effort. *This isn't real. I'm dreaming. This is my sub-conscious playing tricks on me. Any minute now I'm going to wake up on the patio at Nick's, having just met David. My glimpse has become a nightmare and now it's over. There's no place like home. There's no place like home. There's no place like home. Maybe I should attempt to kick my feet together.*

Landon is leaning over me again, "So, you cannot remember anything?" He rocks back on his heels and laughs bitterly, "Fuck, that works out just peachy for him doesn't it?

You cannot remember a goddamn thing he's done to you and he looks like a fucking saint."

I look at him puzzled, the pounding in my skull growing steadily worse.

I rub my temples in an attempt to ward off the pain, "What in the hell are you talking about?"

Maybe I should tell him none of this is real and that we just need to wait it out. It's almost over. It can't get any worse and just like that, the memory floodgates open and I'm so incredibly angry that it was Landon who held the key the entire time. Now I realize why Dr. White lied to me earlier today. This is too much for one person to deal with.

The brain is so complex and for whatever reason after the car wreck, mine decided to create an alternate reality. A reality where I was not the most disgusting, abhorrent creature to ever walk the face of this earth.

PART THREE: REMEMBERING

CHAPTER TWENTY-FIVE

Memories come flowing out, but a lot of the details are still fuzzy. It's like a movie you've seen one time. You can recall the highlights of it, not necessarily every scene. Let me start by saying that I'm not a serial killer. I feel that it's important to get that out in the open. Perhaps, I should back up a bit and explain myself.

I grew up in a loving home, the only child to two wonderful parents. I was by no means spoiled—I didn't get everything I wanted and I was expected to make my own way. While they didn't support me financially, they were there for me emotionally as best they knew how to be.

I was twenty-one when I met Jess. I worked at the local grocery store close to campus almost every evening to pay my way through college. Normally, they let me do the book-keeping—which was perfect for me as I didn't have to interact with anyone other than the manager on duty. I'd arrive at work and they'd lock me in a small room where I'd sit and reconcile every drawer used by the cashiers during the day, making sure that they all balanced out. I'd usually finish up close to midnight and head back to my dorm.

The night I met Jess I'd gotten caught up on counting the tills and Amanda, the manager, asked me to help back-stock as they were down a person. I ended up working next to Jess and we became best friends almost instantly.

I was the quiet to her loud and her personality was so infectious that I would've followed her anywhere. While I was most comfortable in a dark corner booth, being invisible, observing my surroundings, Jess was most comfortable doing shots while standing on top of the bar. She attracted a certain type of guy that way. I would tease her that those kinds of men were vampires—always gone before daylight. I'd always been a bit of an introvert—In all honesty, I didn't put myself out there out of fear of certain rejection later. Being with Jess was like a glimpse into what my life could be like if I was more outgoing. She helped me come out of my shell and always went out of her way to ensure I felt included.

Our footloose and fancy free lifestyle lasted for two years and then she met Nate, a.k.a. "Tattoo Boy". He and I didn't hit it off—to say the least. He wanted her all to himself and I felt that he had a proverbial stick wedged up his ass.

I walked in on a conversation of theirs one time and overheard him ask Jess, "Do you think she's ever going to find someone? I mean, the girl tags along with you constantly. Isn't there anyone we could set her up with?" For a man who was literally covered in tattoos, he sure seemed hung up on appearances.

It did hurt to hear though because I'd often wondered the very same thing. I'd dated some, but it was never anything serious. I wasn't a prude, by any stretch of the imagination. I just saw the relationship my parents had and I wanted something like that before diving in head over heels.

Jess chastised me for having standards that were too high while I worried that hers were non-existent. The thought of being intimate with someone was enough to drive me into a cleaning frenzy to calm myself down. Besides my parents, Jess was the only one to stick around and now it seemed that

Nate was trying to talk her out of it. My anxiety issues were minor at this point, nothing that required therapy or medication.

One night in early 2009, they invited me out to dinner and begrudgingly I went as the third wheel. I wanted to prove to Nate that I was perfectly capable of finding a man, but before our dinner was even served, I'd already rearranged the sugar packets eight different times from nerves. I got up to get another drink and get some air outside—away from all the judgment.

My stiletto became caught in the decking and I fell right into my Daryl Dixon look-a-like, David, dowsing him with pineapple and rum. We didn't actually have our *Walking Dead* conversation though until the show premiered a year later. All I knew was that he was devastatingly handsome and had actually noticed me.

Considering my affinity for risk and danger—sarcasm intended, it's really a big surprise that I fell (literally) for David, with his many tattoos and confident air. He seemed like the ultimate bad boy.

He was twenty-nine and I was twenty-five. There was this magnetism between the two of us, something I'd yet to find with any of the guys my own age. When we kissed, it was electric and I fell hard for him. He was a gentleman and didn't ask me to go home with him that night, but he did get my number and he called me the next day at lunch. He stirred up feelings in me that were confusing and exhilarating at the same time.

We would stay up talking on the phone until the wee hours of the morning—quoting our favorite movie lines, discussing our plans for the future, anything to stay on the phone with each other. We were inseparable after that first meeting.

We went out for pizza one night, not long after we began dating, and we spent hours talking about our lives and how we grew up. Where I'd been shy before, he opened me up and I felt so comfortable in his presence. When they finally kicked us out at closing time, I knew he was the one.

When he took me to a local park with a small pond and got down on one knee a couple of months later, I didn't hesitate for a second. Some might've said it was too soon, but he calmed the storm that raged in my head when doubt took over, and he made me feel so cherished. He was so patient and never seemed bothered by the dark sides of my personality.

I gave him my virginity that night. I just couldn't imagine anyone being more worthy than he was and the two months of foreplay had left me walking around in a constant state of arousal. I'd just wanted everything to be perfect and in that moment, it was. Nate and Jess took to him immediately and Nate became more accepting of me. We weren't close, but David's sense of empathy seemed to be rubbing off on Nate.

David and I had a small wedding on the beach the following May in Galveston, close to his parents. It was everything I wanted and my voice shook as I repeated my vows to him.

"I, Elizabeth, take you, David, to be my husband...to have and to hold...from this day forward...for better, for worse...for richer, for poorer...in sickness and in health, to love and to cherish, forsaking all others, 'til death do us part."

He gripped my hands throughout our recitation of vows, keeping me steady, grounding me.

I'd love to tell you that we got married and he immediately stopped wooing me, but I'd be lying. It happened slowly. While we had our fair share of squabbles over money and household chores, we still shared the same bed every night—nobody ended up in the guest room or on the couch.

However, he was working on growing Greene Construction and there were a lot of late nights and weekends spent away from home. Money ran short and our fighting began to increase. I tried to be supportive and succeeded at first, but it began to feel like every penny was being sucked into his business. What little savings we did have built up began to dwindle under the stress.

By the time 2012 came to a close, I had become a ball of stress. I wanted to be his number one, not some business. Not only was I feeling neglected, but I was becoming increasingly worried about our financial future and what it was he did on those long nights spent away from home.

He said every dime funneled out of savings and into the business was to ensure that our family could live comfortably eventually so that I didn't have to continue working at the dental office after we had children if I didn't want to. It just felt like I was an afterthought to him at that time.

In March 2013, his dad, John, passed suddenly from a heart attack. He'd had rheumatic fever as a young child and it had taken a toll on his heart. Being a strong-willed southern man, he'd refused surgery to repair the damage. He'd always joked that there were going to be droves of devastated women at his funeral when his ticker finally gave out. It was a Saturday and we were sitting on the back patio, a rare weekend that he wasn't trying to finish up a job and we were finally getting some much needed quality time together.

When he got the call, I knew it was bad. He seemed robotic in the disconnected way he told me the news and then he went inside and ran a shower.

I was thrown by his reaction; I'd immediately broken down while he seemed to be on autopilot. When I tried to go into the bathroom to comfort him, I realized the door was locked. I could hear the gut-wrenching sobs as they echoed off the tiles of the shower and I'd never felt so powerless to help him. When he came out of the bathroom, his eyes were dark red and bloodshot. He muttered, "I'm sure going to miss him," as he began packing to go back to his childhood home. As the only child, there was no one else to share his grief in losing a parent and I didn't know how to help him when he insisted on shutting me out.

After the funeral, David was thrust into the role of caring for his mother while she grieved and I felt even more abandoned.

When we got back home, he began taking more out-of-town jobs. When it came to me, his fuse had grown even shorter and it seemed that everything I did set him off. Any time he wasn't working at the company, he was down in Beaumont visiting her. I went from seeing him at night and part of the weekend to not seeing him for weeks at a time. It felt like I was being punished, I just didn't know what my crime was.

I started signing up for volunteer events to occupy my mind and time. That's how I ended up working the health fair in May that year. Landon Scott set up his booth next to mine.

He commanded the room with his presence and I felt my pulse pick up when he looked at me. Having gotten used to being invisible again, I expected him to walk right past my booth.

When he stopped and stood right in front of me, I noticed several women look over at me, clearly wondering what it was about me that drew him in. I wondered the same thing.

Even after he'd introduced himself and then made his way back to his booth he was still trying to engage me in conversation. There was a younger woman in the booth on the other side of me and I struck up a conversation with her when she mentioned despising housework.

"I actually enjoy it. I crank up my music and just get lost in my own thoughts for a while. I know some see it as anti-feminism to be domesticated, but it relaxes me when I'm stressed."

She snorted, "Really? 'Domesticated?' You do realize that's not a word, don't you? —unless you think you're a cat!"

She broke into a fit of giggles and I felt my cheeks burn with embarrassment as I lowered my head. I was wishing I could make myself disappear when a voice spoke up in my defense.

"Actually, it is a word. And it was used in the correct context—something you might know if you ever bothered to pick up a dictionary."

I turned to see Landon leaning on the partition separating our booths before swiveling my head over to catch her reaction—I'm sure she had a name, but it wasn't worth remembering. She stood with her mouth gaping open before beginning three different sentences at the same time. "I was—she said—it was a joke…"

He laughed and ran a hand through his hair before turning back to his booth. All the while she stuttered and stumbled over her words. I gave him a grateful smile.

The rest of the day was spent with me making my way over to Landon's booth anytime the flow of people slowed down just to hear what he would say next. He just drew you in—with the way he became so animated when he told stories.

At the end of the day, we were breaking everything down and Landon offered to take my chair back to the front for me. I handed it to him and when our fingers brushed there was a definite jolt, it gave me chills. I felt my face becoming warm as I blushed when he grinned at me, "You felt that too? Good."

I laughed at myself for thinking that he would've been interested in me romantically. I mean, he'd seen my wedding ring and I'd mentioned that my husband owned his own construction company. I didn't expect anything to come of it until a random encounter a few weeks later changed everything.

It was a Friday that I was expecting David home. He called at five as I was driving to the grocery store to stock the fridge in preparation for our weekend together. He sounded drained as he explained that things had gotten delayed due to the weather and that he would be staying on at least another week until the job was finished.

My heart sank and I began crying so hard that I had to pull the car over. "I haven't seen you in a week! There's no way you could just come home for the weekend?"

He sighed, "Beth, I've been up for nearly thirty-six hours. All I want at this point is to finish this job up and go to bed. I'm not about to drive three and half hours to come home. I just need you to be patient, please. I'm doing this for us." I'd heard that argument before and instead of launching into why we needed to spend more time together, I found I felt much the same way he did—exhausted, drained, and tired of fighting.

"Fuck this, David. Fuck this job and living like this," I struggled to get the words out over my sobs, "I can't do this anymore."

I hung up on him just as a truck cut me off to get into the right turn lane. I was seeing red from my phone conversation and the fucker in front of me just messed with the wrong person. I turned right and sped up before whipping my car in front of his and slamming on my brakes. I laughed as the driver laid on his horn and continued on my way to the store.

A few minutes later, I realized the same truck was tailgating me. I pulled into an empty parking lot and the truck pulled in behind me. Everything in me screamed that I had just done something incredibly stupid and risky, but my rage begged to differ. I jumped out of my car, ready to fight.

"What the fuck is your problem—" The words died in my throat when I realized it was Landon.

He took in my fists at my side and my blotchy face and burst out laughing. "God damn, I thought I'd have to drive all over this city to find you, Elizabeth. I never guessed we'd find ourselves in a road rage incident." His smile was so genuine that I found my anger slipping away just as quickly as it appeared.

"Jesus, Landon, you're a horrible driver!" I smiled at him as I said it and he returned it, dimples on full display.

"Have you been crying?" He approached me cautiously and I took a step forward to meet him.

"It's nothing…just emotional tonight."

"I'm not leaving here until I get your number. I made that mistake before. I mean, I've seen you drive. I wanna make sure you make it home in one piece."

I flipped him off, giggling like a schoolgirl in the process.

Landon had caught me at a point where I was so vulnerable and craving some attention—so instead of refusing to give him my number, I told myself it was just a little harmless flirting. I'd already been worrying that perhaps I'd made a mistake in marrying David. I played the what-ifs over and over again in my head. *What if I said no when he asked me to marry him? What if I didn't let him buy me a drink that night? What if I would've put my foot down on him traveling for work?* It was maddening. I thought having someone I could talk to, one who didn't know David, might really help keep me sane.

I told myself it was platonic and that nothing would come of it. We began texting back and forth throughout the day—nothing that I would be worried about David reading.

He'd check in and see how my work day was going—David wasn't even remembering to do that at the moment. I'd spoken to David every day since I'd met him, but it seemed that he didn't have time to take my calls when he was working now.

A couple of weeks later, after yet another fight, I decided to forego champagne in favor of something stronger. I raided the bar and found a bottle of vodka and five shots later I found myself incredibly aroused and texting Landon.

I expected him to leave after witnessing me vomit, but he helped me into bed and stroked my hair until I fell asleep. I awoke the next morning in bed alone and I cringed at my actions from the night before. Shame brought a flush to my cheeks and I imagined that Landon was probably long gone and in the process of changing his phone number.

It startled me when he walked in the bedroom a few minutes later with two to-go coffees. I pulled the covers up, suddenly feeling modest.

He grinned at me, "How you feeling, champ?"

I groaned and closed my eyes, "I feel like dying…still working out whether it'll be from this hangover or embarrassment."

He chuckled and handed me a coffee before sitting down at the foot of the bed.

"You know, I can't say I've ever made a woman physically ill before," He dodged the pillow I chucked at his head before continuing, "So, now that you're sober would you mind telling me what's going on?"

I swallowed a sip of black coffee before answering him, "Are you sure you wanna hear this? There's still time for you to make your great escape."

His eyes turned serious, "Elizabeth, I haven't been able to get you out of my head since we met. I'm here because I want to be, not out of any sense of obligation."

As we talked over coffee, he asked me about David and I found that I felt safe opening up to him. I shared some of my fears and worries concerning my marriage while he listened quietly. I told him about my anxiety disorder and the debilitating attacks I sometimes suffered. He didn't try to solve my problems or even speak ill of David and I had to admit, it felt good to get some of it off my chest.

Landon genuinely seemed to enjoy my company. He didn't even try to kiss me before he left that morning— nothing that could be construed as a romantic gesture. He left with the promise that we would get together again soon.

When David told me he was going to head straight from his job in Midland down to his mom's house a few weeks later, I texted Landon to see what he was doing. He invited

147

me over for dinner and I was relieved that I wouldn't be left on my own.

While the layout was similar on our homes, my house seemed cluttered compared to his. He had a neutral beige tone painted throughout the house and the walls were bare. Leather couches and a glass coffee table made up the décor in his living room with a few pictures along the mantle above his fireplace.

One was a picture of Landon and a gorgeous brunette who had to have been at least 5'11. They were standing against some railing with their arms around each other. I gestured to the picture, "She's stunning—let me guess, she's the 'one that got away' and you keep her picture as a reminder of what you've lost."

He laughed as he looked over at her picture. "That's Katya," He said it like "caught ya"—it sounded so exotic. "Her dad is from Russia, so her name is the Russian equivalent of Katie. We dated for a while before she took a job in Denver, so I guess she could've been 'the one' had she stuck around."

I stared, mesmerized by her features. "She looks like she could be a model."

He popped the top of a beer and took a swig, "She was, in college."

Of course she was. I felt a pang of jealousy rise up in me and I had to tamp it down and remind myself that I had no claim on him. I was married and he was just my friend. Regardless of what *When Harry Met Sally* would have the world believe, men and women could be just friends. I just needed to get rid of these emotions—seeing her stirred up some of the old feelings of inadequacy and I could feel the cold fingers of anxiety curling around my throat.

I made an excuse about washing up for dinner as Landon walked out to check the steaks on the grill. I found that I was slightly shaking from my unplanned reaction to seeing Landon's ex-girlfriend. If I wanted the rest of the evening to be enjoyable, I needed to relax and remember that I was married to a wonderful—if albeit, mostly absent man.

This is the point of the story where I should've looked at myself in the mirror and evaluated why I was there. All I saw was a woman desperate for physical affection.

When I came back into the kitchen, Landon offered me a glass of wine, and I accepted it gratefully. There was no way I'd trust myself to drive home under the effects of alcohol, but at the moment I didn't care. I was drawn to him, like a moth to a flame.

Given what had transpired between us a few weeks earlier, I expected our meal to be awkward. I couldn't have been more wrong. Sitting and talking about the inane things we'd done during our work week, I felt comfortable—like it was something he and I had done for years. I found myself easily distracted—mesmerized by his mouth, imagining that he was mine and that we had dinner like this every night.

I lost track of time and realized I needed to get home so I grabbed my purse and walked back into the kitchen where he was washing dishes.

"Landon, thank you so much for dinner. It was nice of you to invite me over. It gets kind of lonely eating alone." I tried to laugh the last part of my statement off as a joke as he pulled me into a tight hug.

He murmured into my hair, "Oh Elizabeth."

I clung to him, the wine was in full effect and I was wet with wanting him. He abruptly stepped back and before I could fully comprehend what was going on, his mouth was on mine. His tongue found its way inside my mouth.

I moaned and he instantly released me, mistaking my pleasure for distress.

"Oh my God—Elizabeth, I'm sorry."

I reached up and brought his mouth down on mine again. Desire flowed through every part of my being and I couldn't tell you if it was the alcohol, him, or a combination of both. Without a word, he picked me up and carried me into his bedroom as I ran my nails up and down his spine. His hands were working to get the zipper down on my dress when he brought me to the edge of the bed. I stood up and shimmied out of it before reaching down to take off my black stilettos.

"Leave them on. Please." He was gazing at me with such intensity that I had to look away, my face flooding with color. He walked closer and tipped my chin up, "Hey. You have nothing to be ashamed of. You're beautiful."

I nodded, too overcome to say anything coherent.

He alternated between removing his clothes with one hand while the other worked to get my underwear off.

"Are you on the pill?" His question pulled me out of my stupor.

"No—David just uses condoms normally."

He stopped me with a finger against my lips, his voice husky, "Hey, I don't need your reasons. I just need to know if you want this," at the word 'this' he gestured between us, "If you do, there's only enough room for me and you here."

While my mind was put off by thoughts of David, my body was filled with a heady desire, ready to be possessed. I quickly pushed him to the back of my mind, along with my inner romantic, who was not at all on board with my decision.

I was mentally thumbing my nose at her when I responded, "Landon, I want you. And this."

He let out a breath he'd been holding and I realized that he wasn't sure how I was going to respond. He grinned wickedly at me, "You're not going to puke on me?" He rolled over and grabbed a condom from his wallet, sliding it over his impressive length.

I shook my head and unhooked my strapless bra, tossing it aside before either of us could change our minds.

Landon managed to utter, "Fuck," before climbing over and forcing his fingers inside of me. "God, you're wet. I want you to come for me." I did, almost instantly, before he picked me up off the bed and pushed me up against the wall, my legs wrapped tightly around him. He used his free hand to pull my hair loose from its bun, while his teeth grazed along my jawline. He buried himself deep inside me and I came apart— it was so unlike anything I'd ever experienced.

I'd love to say that I left immediately, went home, and cried in the shower. Yeah, that didn't happen right away. I participated in more promiscuous activities with Landon, both of us working to memorize every inch of the other's body. I didn't make it home until well after midnight, after telling Landon that what we'd done was a one-time thing— "scratching an itch" if you will— and that we could never do it again. He laughed because he knew that I was lying.

Once I got home, his touch still searing my skin, the enormity of what had happened hit me. I went and sat on the back porch, in shock. I was a cheater and I could never take it back. I could never again say that David was my one and only. When I got cold, I went back inside and began scrubbing the house from top to bottom as if doing so would rid me of my guilt. When that didn't work, I ran a hot bath, scrubbing my skin until it was pink and raw. Then, the tears came.

I looked at myself in the mirror and was disgusted. I'd wanted a male companion to replace David while he was away, how could I have not seen it leading to this? Although I knew that I was ultimately responsible for my actions, I felt rage towards David for pushing me into my current situation.

CHAPTER TWENTY-SIX

When David arrived home a couple of nights later to find me cooking dinner, I was incredibly jumpy. I was certain he would know just by looking at me that I had been with another man. If he suspected anything though, he never gave it away. He actually seemed more content, like the David I knew before he lost his dad. He was healing, it was apparent.

We sat down to dinner and he proudly told me of the work they'd accomplished down in Midland and how big the town was getting with the current oil boom. He spoke of his mother and how she'd asked about me when he was down there visiting. They'd gone through some of his dad's things. When he described how they sat on the floor side by side, alternating between laughter and tears as they relived memories of John, it felt like a knife through my heart.

My sweet, caring husband was dealing with the biggest loss in his life and I'd basically run right into the arms of another man. *What kind of a woman does that?*

I found myself comparing him to Landon. Where Landon looked put-together, David was much more laid back. The word disheveled came to mind, but that seemed a bit critical for the man sitting in front of me. He broke me out of my reverie when he asked me what I'd been up to over the weekend and I lied, saying I held a Netflix marathon on the couch. At that point I still thought what Landon and I had done was a one-night stand—something never to be repeated again. It was best to keep it to myself and chalk it up to a temporary lapse in judgment.

He claimed exhaustion from the long drive and said he wanted to go to bed. I grinned and offered to join him. I'd gotten my fix from Landon and I thought I could go back to being the wife he needed. Plus, I needed to clear my conscience. I needed my husband to drive away my guilt over what had happened. I've read statistics that state women only cheat when they're emotionally finished with their marriages. That wasn't true for me though. I loved David, but he'd been so distant and I just needed to fill that void with another male presence. At least, that's how I justified the entire thing so that I could sleep at night.

When he and I made love that night, the first time since he lost his dad, I really thought we were getting back on track. I felt complete when he was deep inside me.

Having David home seemed to quell the urges and anxiety. I was more relaxed than I had been in months and my encounter with Landon seemed a distant memory.

That is, until a large bouquet of flowers arrived for me at work one afternoon. There were stargazer lilies, various colors and varieties of daisies, and rose. It was gorgeous and my first thought was that they came from David, until I saw the card.

"Elizabeth, I miss you. Can I see you again, please?"

The card was unsigned, but I knew it was from Landon. Lauren looked over, interested, as I crumpled the card in my hand. "Lucky girl, your hubby sending you flowers for no reason?"

I forced a smile onto my face and nodded as emotions warred inside my head. I got up and made my way over to the shredder, feeding the card to its metal teeth. He was supposed to be a one-night stand. So, why was my heart pounding with excitement just from reading his words?

When David left for another job the following Saturday morning, I realized I wasn't going to be able to stay away from Landon. It's funny, once you've had a taste of something forbidden, it's a lot easier to go back to it the second time around.

It was a few nights later after several drinks that I worked up the courage to text him. He'd been quiet since I got the flowers and I didn't know if it was due to some moral dilemma or because he was used to being in control and wanted me to come to him.

"I'm drinking all alone and missing you."

His response was almost immediate.

"Yeah—it must be bad if you're drinking alone. I was just imagining those white lace panties myself. I'm out right now. Can I come by later?"

"I'll be here. Waiting."

I ran a bubble bath and shaved my legs. This is what my marriage was missing; that thrill you get at the beginning of a relationship, the butterflies. You know, the feeling that I thought would last forever with David. A wave of guilt washed over me as I put my underwear on and suddenly nostalgic, I made my way into his closet and found one of his button-up shirts to put on. His scent enveloped me and I climbed into bed, drowsy and missing my husband. I tried brushing a few tears away, but soon realized it was a futile effort.

155

I woke up to a pounding on the front door a few hours later to find it pitch black outside. *How long was I asleep?* I stumbled out of bed, shaky from being awoken so suddenly. I threw open the front door to find Landon.

"I've been calling you for the last two hours. I sent you several texts and you never responded. When you didn't answer, I thought you might be hurt." I looked up into his eyes and realized he'd been drinking...heavily.

I swallowed hard, "I'm sorry. I fell asleep."

His eyes were no longer on mine and were instead taking in my body and I belatedly realized that I never buttoned David's shirt, so my bra and panties were on full display for him. My nipples hardened in response and I was certain he could tell. The hunger in his eyes made me wet and I was at a loss for words. I thought of the woman who'd left him. The woman who'd made me feel so inadequate in comparison. *Your loss, Katya. He loves my curves.*

He walked in, kicking the door shut behind him. I unconsciously took a step back. He was stalking me like I was his prey and I should've been afraid or at the very least, feeling some anxiety. In my addled state, all I felt was need. As he picked me up, my legs instinctively went around him and he stumbled towards the bed. I tasted the alcohol on his tongue and it fueled my desire.

"So beautiful," he murmured as he undressed me. Within seconds, clothes littered the floor and he was inside me, pushing me to the brink. He held my hair in a death grip and effectively silenced my moans by bringing his mouth down hard over mine. It wasn't slow or sweet, yet it was everything I wanted.

Later, we sank back down onto the bed. Landon feathered kisses across my throat and I could feel his heart racing. I was beginning to drift off when he pulled me close to him, crushing me against unforgiving muscle. He whispered into my hair, "Why can't I get you out of my head? You're killing me."

I pulled back to look up at him, surprised, before he continued, "I seriously thought I'd get you out of my system after the first time, but you're all I fucking think about."

"Is that why you're drunk? You're trying to forget me?" My mouth was like cotton.

"You're seriously asking me that? Fuck yes, I've been trying to forget you. I want you, but you're married. You're his and it fills me with rage. I want to possess every part of you and call you mine!"

I sat up, stunned. *This wasn't supposed to happen. It was just sex.* I took a deep breath "Landon, I'm a wreck. You can't want more from me than just sex."

He bolted up as if he'd been shot. "A wreck? You've been put into an impossible situation, but—" he tried to compose his thoughts before continuing, and I could feel the anger rippling off of him, "You know what? You're right. It's just fucking. Let's leave it at that."

He stood up, throwing his clothes on with more force than was necessary. I reached for David's shirt as I was suddenly feeling very exposed. Landon grabbed it before I could and proceeded to rip it down the back before tossing the scraps at me.

I shoved him back against the wall. The alcohol in his system had him unsteady on his feet. He looked down at me, stunned.

"What the fuck is wrong with you?" I hissed, "Do you really think I want to live my life like this? To be married to someone who is never here? To have these feelings for you

157

dominate every part of my life? God, Landon—I can't seem to get you out of my system either, but I'm at a fucking loss on what the next step is here."

He brought his hands up and gripped my hands like a vice. "Damn, you're a lot stronger than you look. Look, I'm sorry—Fuck, I can't think straight when I'm around you."

I stood on my tiptoes, trying to reach his mouth and he released my hands long enough to oblige. There was this electrical current flowing between us when we touched and I worried one or both of us was going to get hurt.

I didn't even attempt to tell myself that it wouldn't happen again. He'd woken something in me and I was quickly becoming addicted to him. We began sleeping together anytime David left town. When he was home, I would throw myself at him out of this fear that he would find me out. I literally had my cake and ate it too.

Landon didn't push me for more, though there were times I wanted that from him. It would've been unseemly to demand more without coming to a resolute decision in my marriage.

I couldn't focus too much attention on it as things were changing rapidly—and not for the better.

I had just walked in from work when I got the text from Jess.

"Lizzie—I need to talk. Something bad has happened."

My response was immediate,

"Jess, what's going on?"

"Nate's gone."

158

"Oh my God—where are you? Are you okay? Of course you're not okay."

"No, I'm not okay. I called into work and I'm at home, getting incredibly drunk."

"Bring me some vodka. I drank everything else."

"Will do, just let me change clothes and I'll be right over."

"Lizzie, I love you. You really are the bestest person I know!"

I laughed to myself, as the texts were becoming more and more incoherent, before going to change. I took another one of David's work shirts off the hanger and a pair of my jeans. It was quickly becoming a pattern.

I arrived within an hour, one hand holding copious amounts of alcohol and the other filled with our favorite DVDs. She snatched the bottle of her favorite vodka out of my hand as I kicked off my shoes and settled onto the loveseat.

Jess chugged vodka directly from the bottle as she recounted finding a text message on Nate's phone the previous night. "It just said, 'Please tell me she's asleep- I need you.' I knew it, I just knew he was screwing around behind my back. The bastard didn't even deny it either. He thinks he's 'in love' with her."

After that bombshell, I made my way into her kitchen and uncorked the bottle of champagne I brought as back-up. Jess gratefully accepted a glass from me as I sank down on the floor next to her.

159

I took a few sips of the cool, bubbly liquid in an attempt to make sense of what she was telling me. We sat in silence, both of us completely in shock.

"Jess, I am so sorry. I know that I'm going to break the friend code by saying this, but you know I have never liked him. I still can't believe that shit was cheating on you though."

She alternated between the vodka and champagne, remaining silent.

"When's the last time you ate something, Jess?"

She sighed, "Maybe yesterday?"

"God, Jess that is super unhealthy. You're eating tonight—end of discussion."

We'd ordered a pizza and gotten most of the way through *Bridesmaids* when Nate texted her. Once she read it, she began to look a little green. Being the good friend that I was, I held her hair back as she vomited.

CHAPTER TWENTY-SEVEN

After dealing with the situation with Jess, I managed to put some distance between myself and Landon. I'd be lying if I said it wasn't difficult. David had reverted back to being aloof and I felt like I was being locked out of my own marriage. When I mentioned therapy, he'd looked genuinely offended and I'd ended up changing the subject to keep him placated.

I really thought that maybe David and I were destined to live the rest of our lives as roommates until one of his employees became a dad.

When we went over to the hospital to see his little girl, I saw something in David that frightened me. Soon, all he began talking about—when he was home, was how he couldn't wait to be a dad. I knew he was imagining his own dad and the things they did together when he was growing up and he wanted all of those things for a little one of his own.

While I'd wanted to have children eventually, the thought of balancing work with a screaming newborn and a husband who was gone the majority of the time frightened me. I could barely take care of myself, yet I told him I wanted all of those things too. What else could I have done—tell him I was scared senseless and possibly set him off?

We decided to start trying when he finished up his next job and the minute he left to go back to work, I made a phone call to Jess. She answered rather sleepily on the third ring.

"H-hello, Lizzie?"

I cringed, "Sorry to wake you, Jess. How are you doing?"

"I've given up sleep in favor of becoming," she yawned heavily, "an alcoholic. What's going on?"

"I feel really silly for calling you now. You get some rest and we'll talk later."

"Lizzie Greene, you did not just wake me up to see how I am. Start talking or so help me—I will do something."

"Well, David has got it in his head that he needs to be a dad. Now, he's said that we'll start after his next job. I'm just—I'm just not ready for this. He's not home enough, you know?"

I heard another yawn and thought she might have dozed off while I was talking so I was startled when I heard her voice. "He's not thinking correctly right now. He's still grieving his dad and he thinks a baby of his own will help. If you really don't feel like you can talk to him, then you'd better get on the pill.

I made an appointment with my OB/GYN and she prescribed birth control pills. I wasn't ready to be a mom, at least not until my husband worked through some things and took jobs closer to home.

David went out and picked up a pregnancy test when my period was late a few weeks later and I held my breath during the longest three minutes of my life. I counted backward and realized that I hadn't even waited until the pills were effective before we were having unprotected sex. I had to feign disappointment when it came back negative.

After that, I thought things would go back to "normal", but the pregnancy scare brought my anxiety out in full force and I felt like a bowstring taut and ready to snap at the slightest thing. I was a complete train-wreck.

It was becoming too much to manage between my work obligations, David coming home just to try to knock me up, and Landon constantly checking in to see how I was. I needed someone to talk to—Jess was either drunk or sleep-deprived. Her advice stopped making sense when she suggested I work-from-home making delicious smoothies with the Vitaminja Pro Series Blender. Not only could it whip up smoothies and shakes, but toss in an entire meal and it would cook the whole thing in thirty seconds or less. I worried that she was getting the majority of her advice from late-night infomercials and decided to call a professional.

I lied to David and told him that I was struggling with my inability to get pregnant and he suggested I see a therapist. I scheduled an appointment with Dr. White on the following Monday afternoon when he was out of town.

CHAPTER TWENTY-EIGHT

My first meeting with Dr. White was slightly different now that I remember it as it happened. I sat on the couch while she sat across from me in her plush red velvet armchair, her legs tucked up underneath her.

She began, "Elizabeth, I need you to walk me through this situation you're in. How did it all start?"

I swallowed and began, "My husband, David, is gone a lot. The jobs around here have dried up lately, so he's been traveling all over the state—taking whatever comes his way," She just made notes and listened without judgment and even passed me some tissues when I choked up. "I know I should be supportive, but it's really been taking a toll on us lately. Since he lost his dad he's taken on even more work for himself and when he's not working, he's with his mom."

Once the floodgates were opened, hurts I didn't even know existed began to pour out. "I just feel abandoned emotionally by David. He's thrown up these barriers and it doesn't matter what I do—I can't break them down. I've lost!" I try in vain to dry my tears with the tissue, but they just kept coming.

Dr. White looked up at me, "Elizabeth, if you've lost—who has won?"

I sniffled, "David is just gone, like he can't even stand to be around me anymore."

She gave me a sympathetic smile, "You are in charge of you. You cannot let another person dictate your life," She let me regain my composure before continuing, "Let's talk more about David and your feelings of abandonment there."

"Since his dad died, he's shut me out emotionally while he's dealt with things and it hurt," I paused to try to pull myself together, "Now, he's so focused on building his business and checking in on his Mom every other weekend that I feel like I never see him."

Dr. White nodded at me, "And what is his plan for the business? Is he going to be bringing in more help?"

I sighed, "I think that his ultimate plan is to grow the business enough to step back some, but right now he's basically married to his company. When you hear people talk about how hard it is to be self-employed, they aren't kidding. His phone rings constantly and there's always a sub-contractor that's not showing up or doing their job incorrectly when they are there."

She noted my response, "Has he mentioned where you fit into this grand plan?"

I snorted, "No, he just tells me to be patient. I've tried, but now he wants a baby—I'm scared. Financially, things have already been tight and if he and I are already on shaky ground—how bad will our lives be with a newborn?"

"Did you express your hesitation to him?"

Her last question caught me slightly off-guard, "No, he's had such a rough year with losing his Dad and having to look for bigger jobs out of town. I guess I didn't want to add to his stress—he's so hard right now, but there's this vulnerability about him too. And I did want to have a baby, but the thought of being the only one responsible for caring for it scares me. Look at what a bang up job I'm doing with just me." I gave a self-deprecating laugh, but she didn't seem amused.

"How are you coping?"

"I've cleaned the house a lot and—I met someone," Dr. White tilted her head and raised her eyebrows at me. "It's not like you're thinking. He and I met at a job fair a couple of months ago and he became a friend. Landon has been the only one to care enough to ask about my day and what's going on with me." Never mind the fact, that I had slept with him on multiple occasions, I wasn't quite ready to divulge that information to a stranger.

"Elizabeth, you mentioned that you've been cleaning a lot and that seems to be your coping mechanism for stressful situations, but I also want you to look at it symbolically. Do you think that you cleaning until your home is spotless is an effort to remove the guilt you feel over your marriage having problems?"

"I guess so, but the thing with Landon isn't like that,"

She stopped me, "I'm not even specifically referring to Landon. You have anxiety and control issues—and right now, your marriage is the thing over which you have the least amount of control."

I'm sure my mouth hung open. "I hadn't even looked at it that way, but it's true. I feel powerless and to be honest, I'm tired of fighting."

She nodded in agreement with me. "You're so much more than what's happening in your marriage. Don't let the status of one area of your life define you as a person. Life isn't a movie. Prince Charming doesn't rescue the princess from an ordinary life only to live 'happily ever after'. All relationships can become stale and ordinary over time unless you work at them and they all go through rough patches. You probably find yourself attracted to Landon because he recreates the feelings you had for David when you met—and he makes you feel valued."

I frowned, "I understand that real life is not a fairy tale, and I feel like my Prince Charming did rescue me—from myself. It's just lately though, that I feel like I've been dropped over the side of a cliff while he yells, 'Sorry—you'll have to save yourself now!' I feel like I got ripped off. Landon is exciting in that he pays attention to me and cares about what's going on in my life, I don't have those kinds of feelings for him though." In reality, my words couldn't have been farther from the truth. No need to admit to anything now though.

She tapped a finger against the side of her journal. "While I believe it is unintentional, this behavior is self-harming. You are setting yourself up for a very big fall and I don't know that emotionally you'll be able to handle it when the time comes. Are you willing to risk losing your marriage and most likely your friends for a 'relationship' with Landon? And what if he's only in this because of the thrill of being with a married woman?"

I was dumbfounded, "I don't know, I haven't even considered leaving my marriage. He's just been a friend. I love David." I grabbed another tissue as a fresh round of tears began.

"I'd like to put you on some anxiety medication. It just seems highly impulsive for you to seek out a new friendship, especially with a member of the opposite sex. Medication might help with handling the anxiety

"I don't know that I need to be medicated—I don't think that my friendship with Landon began on impulse." I was uncomfortable with where this was going. I began chewing on my lower lip and tried to focus my attention on the large clock hanging on the wall behind her head.

She regarded me thoughtfully, "I want to place you on medication temporarily and I want you to promise me you'll take it. I know I cannot tell you what to do, but I think it would be in your best interest to sever contact with Landon for the time being. You need to step back and re-evaluate the path you're choosing. Inside of you there is a stronger woman, waiting to rise from the ashes—one whose value isn't tied to any man."

I left her office after promising to follow her instructions and we made an appointment for the following week. I took the rest of the afternoon off to try and sort my thoughts. My phone alerted me to a text when I pulled into my driveway. It was David.

"Beth, how'd it go at your appointment? I hope she gave you some good advice. Just wanted you to know I miss you and I'm thinking of you."

My eyes filled with tears. Maybe the impenetrable fortress he'd built around himself was coming down.

I replied to him.

"It went well. Thanks for checking in on me. I'm counting the days until you get home. Love you more."

CHAPTER TWENTY-NINE

I'd managed to avoid Landon's texts for the first two weeks after my appointment. I didn't know how else to deal with him. I started on my medication and was working on journaling my feelings. Most of the time, I'd write my thoughts down and then immediately run them through the shredder, paranoid that someone would find and read them.

David started coming home every Friday evening and staying until Sunday. I felt like I was finally regaining some semblance of stability in my life.

Jess was mostly unavailable, dealing with her divorce. We were still texting on and off, but thankfully, she'd given up on me quitting my job to open my own smoothie bar.

Landon showed up unexpectedly at my house on a Wednesday evening. David wasn't due in for two days and I had fallen asleep on the couch. I could tell he was frustrated when I opened the door. "I've been trying to reach you for the last two weeks. I was worried about you when I didn't get a response. Are you okay?" His voice caught and I thought I saw a tear in the corner of his eye.

"I'm fine—I'm sorry. My therapist said I needed to take a break from," I gestured to him, "this. I think she's afraid of that line becoming blurred."

He sank onto the arm of the couch. "She's right. I know how it must seem—a single man and a married woman—look, there's another reason I stopped by. Katya is moving back to Lubbock and we've reconciled. It's probably better if we don't talk after tonight, but I couldn't walk away without explaining why. You deserve that much."

I felt as though a knife had been twisted in my gut and I had to remind myself that I'd wanted this to happen. I'd wanted Landon to meet someone that made him happy because I could never imagine my life without David. I struggled to clear my thoughts.

"I'm happy for you, Landon. Really, I am. You're a great guy—you've been my rock over the past six months, but maybe it is time we went our separate ways."

We hugged each other and then he was gone while I was left to sort out the confusing feelings he'd left me with.

Things were pretty much the same over the next month; with the exception that David was becoming more frustrated by my inability to become pregnant. I knew he was beginning to think one or both of us might have fertility issues.

We began to bicker about it when he was home until I lost it one night. He was sitting on the couch researching fertility clinics in the area when I finally worked up enough courage and reached into my purse before tossing the birth control pills onto his lap. I whispered, "This is why we're not getting pregnant," and braced myself for the storm that was inevitably coming. He stared dumbly at the plastic packet before slowly looking up at me. He stood up and while his voice remained eerily calm, he didn't mince words.

"What the hell is wrong with you, Beth? Why would you do this? What else have you been lying about?"

"David, please, it's not like that,"

"Oh Beth, then enlighten me, by all means." His voice had taken on a sarcastic tone.

I pressed my fingers to my eyes, willing the tears to ease up so I could speak. "You've just taken on all these jobs out of town. You want to start a family, but you're never here. Since you lost your dad, it feels like everything I do is wrong in your eyes. I didn't want to admit I wasn't ready to have a baby and have you more disappointed in me. I'm so sorry, David."

He shook his head in disgust and without saying anything further, grabbed his keys off of the island and went out to the garage. I heard his truck roar to life as he backed out of the driveway. Then he was gone, the red taillights of his pick-up the only thing visible in the inky darkness outside. I sat on the couch and wept. I was so tired of fighting and lying every month when the tests came back negative.

Now, I needed to prepare myself for divorce papers as it was inevitably going to happen. *Maybe I should Google "Divorce in Texas".* Marriages had ended over less than this. We hardly saw each other and when we did; his phone was the only thing interrupting our arguments. I heard him stumble in some time later and head down the hall to the guest room. I pulled the covers up over my head, burying myself and my regrets under them.

When he approached me with an envelope a few days later, I had to bite back a sob—I knew it was divorce papers. I was completely taken aback when I realized that there were two tickets to Cabo San Lucas inside. "Beth, I know we didn't get to celebrate our anniversary back in May with everything we had going on, and we're going through a bit of a rough spot right now, but I really think a getaway would be good for us." He left it at that, with no mention of me being on birth control. It seemed as if he wanted to forget the fight even happened.

171

We spent a week in Cabo with no cell service and I realized why I fell in love with him. He was so incredibly intelligent and could make me laugh so easily. Being with him like this was comfortable and it made our problems back home seem easily solved. When I had him, one hundred percent, I felt like we were unstoppable.

When we got back, David and I spent the holiday season with family and friends. He made a conscious effort to take more jobs in town during this time so we became accustomed to seeing each other again every night.

We spent a lot more time together and I found myself becoming more open to the idea of having a baby together. I talked to him about it and we both decided I should stop taking my birth control pills in February so we could start trying.

That's not to say that it was all sunshine and rainbows. Money was still a big concern, with David bringing home huge paychecks one month and nothing for the next.

March brought more out of town jobs and I began to see less and less of my husband. At Dr. White's urging, I brought my concerns up to David only to be met with resistance, "If we're going to have a baby, I need to take these bigger jobs to cover those costs. Please understand, I'm doing this for us!" I felt as though I would splinter from the back and forth between us, yet I recognized how hard he was trying to make us work.

Every night consisted of the same thing, *David deserves better. David deserves more than this. You deserve more than this.* I repeated it over and over in my head until exhausted from the emotional stress, my body slipped into a dreamless sleep.

Jess picked up on my distractedness and questioned me on it. I lied and told her I was having a hard time dealing with my inability to get pregnant and missing David. She didn't seem convinced, but let it go.

Such a tangled web we weave.

I also felt like I was going through the motions at work while my mind tried to compartmentalize everything that was going on in my personal life. It didn't take long for Lauren to notice. She confronted me by the copier one day.

"Who died?"

I looked at her, "What are you talking about?"

She was clearly becoming frustrated, "You! You walk around here like you're in a dream and I figure someone you love must be dying."

I lowered my voice, "Look, I don't want to talk about it here. Can we go to lunch somewhere?"

She nodded, "Sure, let's do that. Now, I really need you to get back to work. We've got an issue with the schedule for next Wednesday. Doc's going to be out so we'll need to move those appointments." *How could I let my personal life get in the way of next Wednesday's schedule?* I managed to keep my snarky remark to myself—just barely.

We sat across from each other in a nearby deli after a whirlwind of a morning at work. I'd just spilled my guts to Lauren and, to be honest, she looked a little shell-shocked.

"How—why? I don't understand. I thought you and David were happy."

"We were—he's just been out-of-town five days a week and I've been lonely. I don't even know how to begin cleaning up this mess. I don't want to call up Landon, but my husband won't return my calls."

"You have your friends here to help you. I want you to take the rest of the week off and sort this out. I'll cover for you." She seemed so determined that it rattled me.

173

"Why are you being so nice to me? I didn't think you liked me all that much?"

"Of course I like you! You're my friend. I know I can be hard on you, but it's because I know how much you're capable of. Let me help you—anytime that you're thinking of texting or calling Landon, reach out to me instead and I'll drop everything."

I debated telling her about how I've been using her contact as a cover for Landon already, but decided against it. Hey, she just admitted that she liked me, no need to burn that bridge immediately.

CHAPTER THIRTY

I awoke the next morning to a text from Lauren,

"Hey, just had a thought. Why don't we grab dinner tonight? I'd offer to cook for you, but you know that I don't know my way around a kitchen. So, you pick and I'll meet you there."

I smiled and quickly responded,

"I'm in! Meet you at Crafthouse around 7?"

"Perfect—it's a date."

I saw that I had a missed call and voicemail from my mother as well.

"Sweetie, it's your mom. Listen, I heard the oddest rumor today. Your dad and I were getting groceries when we ran into Shirley. You remember Shirley; we play cards together once a month. Well, she said that she heard from her neighbor, Jean, that you were out without your wedding ring and with a man who is most certainly not David. I told her she was mistaken; that our little girl would never do that. I do hope you're being good to David. Anyway, call me back and let's get together for brunch next Sunday-the four of us. It's really been too long."

When Landon and I were together, we'd gone to late movies and obscure bars where the odds of us being recognized were slim. We'd met for coffee once, the most public thing we ever did—I guess it took the rumor mill long enough to circulate that news back to my parents. Just when you think it can't get any worse. Now I remember why my parents despise me.

I got dressed for dinner and tried not to think of the voicemail my mother left. I tried singing along to my favorite songs, meditative breathing—it wasn't working. How's that saying go? I have ninety-nine problems and ninety-two of them are made up scenarios in my head that haven't even happened, yet I'm freaking out for no logical reason—*I think that's right.*

What if she calls David? What if this all falls apart even though I ended it with Landon? What if they hate me and disown me? I turn the music up louder in an effort to drown out my thoughts.

I made it to the restaurant a few minutes before seven and found a cozy booth back in the corner. Lauren walked in a couple of minutes later. After glancing over the menu, she looked up at me.

"So, you never told me how you ended it with Landon or how he reacted."

I glanced around to make sure no one heard her. "I just ended it. I quit calling him when David and I got back from Mexico. He showed up one night after we got back."

She gasped and then glared at me.

"Before you get upset, nothing happened. He wanted to let me know that his ex-girlfriend was moving here. It was pretty apparent he thought we were through. I knew it was coming, I can't say it didn't hurt though."

She opened her mouth as the server came and took our drink orders. We both ordered unsweetened iced teas. She waited until he was gone. "So, Landon was just fine with everything being over? From what you've told me about him, he doesn't seem like the type to just be done."

176

I started picking at my paper napkin ring, "He could be very intense at times, but he's in love with his ex. He made that pretty clear."

She lowered her voice, "Elizabeth, the guy calls you repeatedly for two weeks only to tell you he's not into fucking you anymore? You swear that you didn't hook up for old time's sake?"

I was given a temporary reprieve when the server brought our drinks out. After informing him that we needed a few extra minutes, Lauren turned her gaze back to me, "Let's go, Greene. No more stalling."

"I swear, Lauren. Nothing happened. You're right and I'm going to be a better person, even if it kills me."

She laughed, "If I have to move in with you when David's out of town to keep you safe, I'll do it."

We finally ordered food, much to our server's delight and Lauren began teasing me about David. "So, have you ever gotten him to dress all grungy and posed him with a cross-bow in his hands? I think you need a picture of that for your desk."

We collapsed in a fit of laughter and I found that I was truly looking forward to spending more time with her. We parted with plans to meet at the gym the following night so Lauren could get me into "fighting shape" as she called it.

I realized when I got into my car that I'd lost track of the time and it was almost ten. I also saw three missed calls from my mother. She was persistent. I bit the bullet and called her back.

She answered on the second ring, "Elizabeth? Honey, please tell me what's going on, It isn't like you to avoid my calls."

I swallowed the lump in my throat, "Hi, Mom. I'm fine. It's just been a little rough lately."

It was so quiet on the other end of the line that I was worried that my cell phone dropped the call. "—Mom?"

I heard a small sigh, *was she crying?*

"I'm here. I'm so sorry… we had no idea you two were having problems. It's true then? Are you having an affair?" She was crying so hard that the last word came out as a squeak.

"Mom, calm down. Let's get together and talk—not over the phone, please."

I pulled into my driveway and opened the garage.

"Elizabeth Marie, you tell me the truth. I deserve that much."

I walked into the house and kicked my heels off in the kitchen before heading into the bedroom to get out of my dress. I took a deep breath, "Mom, it's not what you think. It was a mistake and it's over now." Instead of heading into my closet for a t-shirt, I made my way into David's closet. Just breathing in his scent calmed me down and I chose the denim pearl snap shirt he wore the night we met and put it on over my underwear.

"—Mom? Please say something."

She sniffled again, "I'm just shocked…"

I opened up my closet to hang up my dress and then left the bedroom. I wasn't even listening to my mom anymore as I walked into the living room and switched on a lamp. The curtain on the front window was flapping in the evening breeze. I hadn't left any windows open when I left for dinner. My heart began to race. *Someone was in the house. And they didn't bother to hide that fact. Take a deep breath—in and out.*

I tried to keep my voice steady, "Mom, I have another call coming in. I'll call you back in the morning and we'll plan a time to sit down. Just—don't call David, please."

After ending the phone call, I began going room to room, checking every window. The back guest room window was shattered and it gave me chills knowing that someone had free reign inside my house without me being there. *I need to call the cops. I need to see if anything's been taken. Thank God I watch Investigation Discovery so I know these things.*

I pulled my cell phone out of the shirt pocket and stared at it blankly for a moment. I needed to text Lauren, but I was struck with the fear that I'd been texting Landon earlier. I checked the numbers and realized I was actually texting Lauren. *Could he have broken in?* Who else would have known I was out to dinner? *Someone's watching me.*

I called David and he answered on the second ring, "Hey, did I wake you?"

"No, I'm up. What's wrong?"

"I came home from dinner," I paused and swallowed the lump in my throat, "And the back bedroom window was shattered."

"Beth, was anything stolen? Please tell me you're not in the house right now."

I bit my bottom lip and stared at the glass on the carpet. I couldn't very well tell him that I suspected it was someone I'd been intimate with. I did a cursory glance around the room and walked back to the living room.

"No, it looks like everything is here and yes; I'm still in the house."

"Beth, listen to me. I want you to go get in your car and lock the doors. I'm going to call Mike and see if he can't head that way. Have you called the police? Maybe he's on shift tonight."

"Not yet."

"Okay, I want you to call them the minute we hang up. I'm going to pack up my stuff and I'm coming home."

I was going to protest, but I was really shaken. I needed my husband.

CHAPTER THIRTY ONE

Several police officers showed up within ten minutes. I closed the front window, before changing into sweat pants and a tank top. Looking back, I should've left everything as it was, but I was shaken up and nothing I seemed to be doing was rational anyway.

Mike was there within five minutes. He and David grew up together and were inseparable. With his surfer boy good looks and witty personality, it was hard to believe he was single. He wrapped a blanket around my shoulders and sat next to me on the couch while the two officers checked the house and yard.

The female officer walked back inside. She was petite with beautiful long red hair and a face that made it clear she didn't take any crap from anyone. She glanced at Mike and then sat down on the ottoman in front of me. "Mrs. Greene, you're sure nothing has been taken?"

"No, I don't think so. I didn't notice anything of value missing. I just came home and the back window was shattered." My teeth were chattering together so hard that I feared they might chip.

She looked at Mike, "Detective Sullivan, could I have a word?"

Mike reached over and placed his arm across my shoulder, a protective move that I greatly appreciated. "Anything you've got for me can be said in front of her."

The other officer walked back in with something rectangular in his hands. He held it up for me to see, "Does this look familiar?"

My heart leapt into my throat, "That was the frame for a picture from our wedding day. Where's the picture?"

Mike interjected, "Did you dust that for fingerprints?"

The officer gave him a pointed look, "We did and recovered nothing. It was right outside that back window. We've checked everywhere inside and out and cannot find evidence that anyone was here," He turned back to me, "We didn't find a picture. Just the empty frame."

After assuring me that they would file the report and follow up on any leads, both officers left. Mike got up and went and grabbed two beers out of the fridge. I took a sip and placed mine on a coaster, while trying to calm my mind.

Whoever was inside my house knew enough not to leave anything behind. I wasn't even sure what kind of crazy I was dealing with in this case.

"Elizabeth, are you okay?"

I snapped back to reality, "Yeah, just trying to figure out who would've done this and why."

He took a drink of his beer. "Yeah, it's not normal by any stretch of the imagination. It's like it was done just to prove they could get in, unless something scared them off."

I nodded, an icy cold was wrapping around my gut. This person wanted to scare me—*but why?*

I began crying and Mike pulled me to his chest. "Hey now, it's going to be fine. David's going to be here in the next couple of hours. Just relax; you've been so strong dealing with this." I placed my head on his shoulder and tried to calm down.

He ran his hands up and down my back as if he was trying to warm me up. I closed my eyes and focused on my breathing. *He smelled so good—like shaving cream and cologne. He smells like David.* With that thought, the tears came back full force.

"Why don't you go try to get some sleep and I'll stay on the couch until David gets in."

I nodded and stood up, "Thanks, Mike."

He gave me a sad smile and I went into the bedroom, closing the door behind me. The overall stress from the evening seemed to be rearing its ugly head and I barely made it to the bathroom. *Why do I hold stress in my gut?* I splashed cold water on my face before rushing over to the toilet and emptying my stomach.

My stomach had just finished its revolt and I lay with my face against the toilet seat when I felt a cold washcloth against the back of my neck. I glanced up to see Mike.

"You've had an incredibly stressful evening and now you're sick? You poor thing."

I managed a weak smile, "Pretty sure you would've preferred to spend your evening in a more relaxing manner."

"Not when my best friend's wife is in trouble. Let's get you into bed." He helped me up and into bed before going back to the couch. I really needed a do-over for the last year.

My cell phone chirped in bed next to me. I put my glasses back on and saw that it was from Lauren.

"Hey would you be interested in trying out a class at the gym with me tomorrow?"

I smiled,

"As long as it doesn't have the potential to kill me...sure."

I debated whether or not to tell her about the break-in, but my eyes were heavy and I soon fell into a fitful sleep.

I awoke to David closing the bedroom door behind him. He climbed in next to me and pulled me into his big warm body. "It's okay, Beth. I'm home now."

I nestled my head in the crook of his arm while hot tears ran down my face. I was so scared.

Please don't leave me. Please don't leave me.

I managed to stifle my sobs, "David?"

He leaned down to me, "Yeah?"

"I-I'm glad you're home."

I awoke the next morning to find David making us breakfast in the kitchen. Mike was gone and I'd already missed four calls from my mother. I kissed him good morning and then gestured to my phone, "I need to call my mother back. I've missed several calls."

He nodded at me and went back to scrambling eggs while I stepped out onto the back patio. She answered by the second ring.

"Hello?"

"Hi Mom, it's me. I saw I missed some calls from you."

She snorted sarcastically, "Yeah, I was just calling to chat, see if you wanted to grab lunch—why do you think I was calling, Elizabeth? I find out my daughter is cheating on her husband and she can't even be bothered to explain herself!"

I cringed and lowered my voice, "Mom, I-I know how it must seem, but it's over—I told you that last night. It was a horrible mistake."

"We raised you better. David is a good man—how could you do that to him—after everything he's been through?" Her voice was getting louder and louder the angrier she got.

"Mom, please—I'm sorry. I'm trying to be a better person. I'm not that person. I've been seeing a therapist and I really think she can help me work through this."

"Oh my God—David has remained so strong throughout losing his dad and nearly his business and you—you run off and have your little 'therapy sessions', but don't think twice about sleeping with another man during this time. I don't know who you are anymore."

I gasped more from shock than hurt. Everything she'd just mentioned, I'd thought about myself. She, however, wasn't through with me yet.

"And let me be the first to say that when David finds out about this, which he will, no one will think unkindly of him if he leaves you. I've held my tongue for far too long—but you have brought this on yourself. You go out of your way to make yourself difficult to love with these dramatics. Your father and I supported you with your anxiety issues, but this—this behavior is nothing more than a temper tantrum. Adults don't do that, Elizabeth. They don't run out and sleep with another man because their spouse is taking too long to grieve."

I reeled back from my phone as though I'd been slapped. My mother was never harsh like this with me. She was many things, but never harsh.

I wiped my tears and put the phone back against my ear.

"—that's what happens when you rely on your spouse as your source of happiness. You end up disappointed when they inevitably slip up and then you end up trying to find a new source of happiness. If you would just choose to be happy and not make it contingent on another person, your life would be so much better."

185

I sighed and said sarcastically, "You're so right, Mom. If I could just choose happiness, my life would be rainbows and sunshine—like anyone would choose to live like this!"

I hit the 'end' button and sank down in the patio chair.

"What the hell was that?"

I jumped about three feet in the air and turned to find David standing behind me with two plates of food in his hands. *Oh God—how long has he been standing there?*

"I-she-I—you heard that?" *That was smooth.*

"You're damn right I heard it—attacking you for going to therapy? That's a low blow. I know you want to be happy— you can't let your mom make you feel bad about yourself."

That's right—wait. What?

He set the plates down roughly and turned back to me. "Is she always like this to you? Judging you? Making you feel bad about yourself?"

Moment of truth—if I lie, I'm ruining the relationship with my parents. If I tell the truth, I'm going to lose the man I love.

I brushed some more tears away. "She has a hard time understanding me, I think. She means well, but she thinks it's nothing more than 'temper tantrums'. I don't know, maybe she's right."

Well, I did it. I threw my mother under a bus and watched as it bounced over her body. Some daughter I am. In my defense, I didn't really have a lot of choices if I wanted to save my marriage. I glanced at David through tear-stained lashes.

"What do you want to do, Beth? Do you want to continue to allow her to determine what's best for your mental health?" He brought his fist up and placed it against his mouth as if doing so would hold back his anger.

"I don't know. I think I need some distance right now."
Inwardly, I sighed. *I'm sorry, Mom. But if I'm going to keep David from finding out, I have to keep him far, far away from you.*

CHAPTER THIRTY-TWO

David and I ate our breakfast in silence. I sipped my coffee, wishing for something stronger while I dealt with thoughts of my parents.

"I brought in some help to finish that job down in Midland. I've decided that I need to stick with local jobs from now on. I won't be bidding on any out-of-town work."

I'm jolted back to reality by his words. I stared open-mouthed at him while holding my coffee cup to my lips.

"Is this because of what happened last night?"

"No. Beth, you're the most important thing in the world to me. I've been traveling all over for work and I just miss the hell out of you. I had already set this in motion when you called me to tell me what had happened."

It's exactly what I wanted to happen, but I was worried it wouldn't last.

"Haven't we tried this before—after Mexico?"

He looked over at me, while he tried to find the right words to say.

"Look, Beth—I know that the jobs here have been smaller, but I want us to start a family. If we're ever going to be able to do that, I've got to be here for you. I can't leave you to deal with all of it on your own."

I was floored—sometimes I wondered if he couldn't read my mind. I just felt like I didn't deserve this man. He became animated, gesturing with his hands as he talked about the future. As I watched him, I heard my mother's words come back to haunt me, "*And let me be the first to say that when David finds out about this, which he will, no one will think unkindly of him if he leaves you.*"

I swallowed the lump in my throat and covered his hand with mine. I couldn't imagine my life without David. I stood up and climbed into his lap before pressing my lips to his mouth and down his neck.

"Come back to bed with me?"

He responded by picking me up and carrying me back into the house.

Afterward, I feathered kisses across his neck as he dozed. Then, as I lay my head on his chest and listened to his heart beating, I thought—*this is my husband. Mine.* I realized how right my life was in that moment.

I went through the next few weeks constantly looking over my shoulder. I was so afraid that my mother would pop-up behind me, but my cell phone remained quiet as far as she was concerned. David confronted them and she didn't rat me out, but a part of me was just waiting for the other shoe to drop.

I left work one evening to find Landon waiting by my car. "Hey Elizabeth, long time no see."

"Landon—what are you doing here?"

He shuffled his feet as though he was contemplating his answer, his eyes remained on the pavement, "I just missed you and needed to see you. Katya left." At that, his eyes teared up, and I felt my walls begin to crumble. I couldn't do this. Not again.

"Landon, I'm sorry to hear that—but I've got to get home to David. I'm sorry."

He held his hands up, "I get it—I do. I just wanted to see you." He pulled me into him and whispered, "Plus that skirt and I have history. You know I can't think clearly when you're wearing it."

I glanced down at my black skirt and the May air suddenly felt a little too cool for me. I pulled away from him and wrapped my arms around myself to stop the shaking. "I've got to get home, Landon. Good to see you."

He nodded sadly and gave me a forced smile. "Take care, Elizabeth."

I went into full-blown panic mode once I arrived home. I began cleaning while waiting for David to get home and when that didn't work, I moved into the kitchen.

David arrived an hour later. "You'll never believe what happened today. I actually met with a prospective client who wanted me to build an addition onto his existing office for—get this—free! I could have a small sign in the front flower bed that said Greene Construction. He said it would be great advertising."

I laughed and turned down my Florence + the Machine Pandora station as he came into the kitchen where I had the oven going and various pots bubbling away on the stovetop.

He took it all in and then walked into the living room as if looking for evidence. "She was here wasn't she?" Seeing my confusion he elaborated, "Your mom—she must've been here. The house is beyond spotless, you've got to be cooking for no less than fifty people over there, and you're listening to Florence—you're stressed or upset."

"Actually, no—it was just a long stressful day at work." David sat down on a bar stool at the island as I began chopping vegetables. "You want to talk about it, Beth?"

I smiled at him, "No, but I'd take a drink."

He poured me a glass of champagne as I began layering the squash, zucchini, and onions in a baking dish with a little more force than was necessary before taking the glass from him.

"Thanks. I just want to finish this and go to bed."

"Wait, what? Are you trying to get me into bed? — because I will totally let you." He grinned wickedly at me as he made his way towards me.

I swatted his arm then sprinkled parmesan and pepper over the veggies before placing the dish in the oven and answering, "I can always be persuaded, but let me finish this up first."

He wrapped his arms around my waist and nuzzled my neck, "I wanna take you out." Sensing my confusion, he amended, "Tomorrow—not tonight. I made arrangements with Jess so you can get your hair done and then she's going to take you shopping for something to wear. Then, the four of us are going out."

I turned to him, my shock evident. "The four of us? Who else is going? What's the occasion?"

He laughed at all my questions, "Well our anniversary is next weekend, but I don't need an occasion. You've been an amazing wife who's had to put up with a lot with me being gone. You deserve this—and Lauren and Mike are coming with us."

I fought against the surge of guilt and images of me with Landon, "I agree. A night out is exactly what we need. Jess didn't want to join us?"

He kissed my cheek. "You know Jess doesn't normally work Saturdays, but for you she was willing to make an exception. I invited her, but she had plans already. Now, that's settled," he lowered his voice to a sexy growl, "I'm ready for my cooking lesson." I was giddy as he picked me up and set me down on the island.

The next morning found me sitting in Jess's chair as she decided what needed to be done. She jumped off of the small stool she'd been sitting on and came over to me. She was in full hairdresser mode at this point and it seemed best to just sit back and let her sell me on her ideas, "What are you thinking you want—extensions? Yes, I am going to make you look so fabulous," seeing the wide-eyed worried look on my face she clarifies, "you'll look classy, I promise. We'll just lighten you up a bit and then give you a little length.

She spun me around to face the mirror once she finished and I barely recognize the woman staring back at me. My simple hairstyle was gone and I now had long layers thanks to the extensions. She'd worked some magic alright.

I began tearing up and Jess stopped me, "No waterworks. This is fun and now, David wants you to go buy a sexy little dress for your night out!"

And that is how I came to find myself in a swank boutique dressing room, trying on dresses that were beyond expensive, and drinking the complimentary champagne like it was water. When I say complimentary, I mean that we went to the liquor store and purchased several mini bottles and smuggled them in to the boutique in our purses. The only thing missing from my "rock star experience" was a straw.

The dress I was wearing at the moment was a slim black number with a plunging neckline. It was going so well until I saw the price tag-$1560? I felt sick.

My phone chirped in my purse, it was a text from David.

"How's it going? Did you find a dress?"

I quickly replied,

"Not quite. I mean I thought so until I saw the price tag on this one. Yikes!"

"Send me a picture. Let me decide if you need it or not."

I snapped a picture and sent it along with the price tag. I knew there was no way he'd go for it. My wedding gown was on a clearance rack, I didn't shop frivolously. I glanced down at my phone as his reply came through.

"You're going to need a pair of shoes to go with that. You deserve this and you never treat yourself. Let me get you some presents. Love you!"

I swallowed the bile in my throat. *Oh David, if you only knew the treats I'd given myself when you were away. I deserve nothing, but hatred from you.*

The feelings of unworthiness consumed me and I barely made it to the bathroom before vomiting in their very expensive sink. I heard a knock at the door as I splashed cold water on my cheeks. "Yes?" I called out a little shakily.

"It's Jess. You okay in there?"

"Yeah, just a little price tag shock—this dress costs more than half my closet!"

She laughed, "Yeah, well someone seems to think you need it. I'm supposed to make sure you leave with that dress and a pair of heels. Get back out here, soldier."

CHAPTER THIRTY-THREE

Lauren came over and she and I were like a couple of teenage girls, as we put on our makeup side by side by side in the guest bathroom. It felt so good to have her here. She warned me to be serious as she lined my lips and I managed to briefly compose myself. "So, Mike. Is he hot?"

I grinned at her, "Oh, he's the hottest and he's a cop!"

"Well, in that case, I'm glad I'm packing!" She reached into her purse and pulled out a roll of condoms. We dissolved into a fit of laughter.

David's voice carried down the hall, "Beth, c'mon. We have to leave no later than seven. You have five minutes."

Lauren mimicked him and we dissolved into giggles again. She turned me toward the mirror and I was amazed. The dress, the hair, and the makeup had all worked together to transform me. I looked like I belonged on the cover of a magazine. "He's going to flip out when he sees you. Girl, you look gorgeous!" Lauren gave me a quick hug and we headed into the living room to greet the boys.

David was in the middle of telling some story to Mike, but he stopped mid-sentence when we walked in. He stood with his mouth open, taking it all in, before giving me an appreciative nod. "Beth, you are just—stunning," He kissed me on the lips before whispering in my ear, "I look forward to seeing you in just those heels later." I hit him playfully and grabbed my purse.

Lauren came to a sudden stop next to me, her eyes glued to Mike. I'd never seen her speechless before. She stuck out her hand, "Hi, I'm Lauren."

Mike looked just as shell-shocked as she did. He gripped her hand, "Mike."

I looked over at David and winked. He was quite the matchmaker it seemed.

I'd expected the four of us to take David's truck, but when I walked out through the garage there was a stretch limousine waiting by the curb. I turned to David, shocked, and he grinned from ear to ear. "Surprise, Beth. Happy Anniversary!"

Lauren began hopping up and down excitedly, "We pulled it off!"

Mike chuckled and I looked at the three of them, "You all planned this? How'd you keep it a secret?" The driver stepped out and opened the door for us as David circled his arms around my waist, "I've got a few tricks up my sleeve. I can keep some things from you."

His words made me uncomfortable as they hit a little too close to home. *So can I, David. So can I.* I shoved the thoughts aside and let him lead me into the limo. I squeezed his hand, "You're awesome, David. I'm blown away."

Lauren and Mike brought enough alcohol for a small army. There was champagne, beer, and flavored vodka chilling on ice. Country music blasted through the speakers and I found I didn't even mind. "Lauren, do you really think we need this much to drink?"

"Are you kidding me? It's the first time I've ever been in a limo, so we are going to take full advantage of that." She popped the top off of two beers and handed one to me before raising hers in the air, "To young love and the best friends a girl could ever want." We tapped our bottles together and settled into the leather seats, the multi-colored interior lights dancing across the glass.

We pulled up outside of *Nick's* and David leaned over to me, "Thought it might be nice to go back to where we started."

Several drinks in—I chose *Malibu* and pineapple for old time's sake, I excused myself to the ladies' room. Lauren and Mike were so into each other; I doubt they even noticed me get up. Afterward, as I made my way back out to the patio, my phone buzzed.

"Nice dress. What's the occasion?"

Landon. My blood ran cold and my eyes began scanning the bar, looking for him. I stepped back into the small hallway and replied.

"You can't text me anymore."

"Yeah, but where's the fun in that?" The voice came from behind me and I jumped. I turned around to find Landon leaned up against the wall, regarding me with a bemused expression.

"What are you doing here? Are you following me?"

He laughed without humor, "Someone thinks a little highly of themselves. I was here first and just happened to see you."

I pushed the fear down and tried to make myself appear taller, "I'm here with my husband so I really don't have time to chat." I turned to leave and he grabbed my arm and roughly pulled me to him, he placed his other hand on my lower back.

"Not so fast, I'm not done with you," He glanced around to make sure no one was watching before dropping his voice, "So Davey-boy is back, huh? Can he make you moan like a

196

whore just by touching you?" His hand slid lower until he was cupping my ass.

I pulled back and turned my head to avoid his mouth. "Get your hands off of me."

I was beginning to panic. His grip on me was tight and any moment now David was going to—

"You wanna get your fucking hands off of my wife or do you need some help?" David was standing there smiling, but his body language showed that he was ready to snap—it made that smile even more unnerving.

Landon quickly released me and stepped back with his hands up. "Sorry man. I've been drinking and she looked like someone I know." I exhaled a breath I didn't realize I'd been holding.

This was my worst nightmare come true. The man I loved and the "other man" in the same room. David pulled me to him and I saw that Lauren and Mike were directly behind him. Mike stepped forward in case David needed back up.

Landon turned his gaze on me, "I'm really sorry ma'am. I meant no disrespect."

His voice dripped with sarcasm, but I didn't think anyone else noticed until Lauren caught my eye. She was looking at the two of us as if she could see right through the lies. I felt like that narrow hallway was getting smaller by the minute.

I was afraid of what Landon would tell David if I left, but I could feel an anxiety attack coming on and didn't really need a crowd to witness that, "I can't breathe." I left David and Landon to their stand-down and went back out onto the patio.

I stood by the railing, looking out onto the small pond and adjacent golf course, willing my body to relax. I felt movement to my left and saw it was Lauren. She reached for my hand, "He's gone. Nobody had to throw any punches. Mike's calming David down now—that was Landon wasn't it?"

I reached into my purse and grabbed my anxiety medication. I popped one in my mouth before taking her drink and swallowing it down. "Lauren, I really don't want to talk about it right now, but yeah, that was him."

"What was he doing here? Did he know you were going to be here?" She was starting to sound as panicked as I was feeling.

I rubbed my temples and sighed, "I don't know why he was here. I didn't start things up again if that's what you're wondering."

I lowered my voice as I said the last part and glanced around.

She regarded me thoughtfully, "I believe you. I just don't understand why he turns up here tonight and what—busts a move on you?"

I'm saved from answering when David and Mike walked back up. David embraced me, "You okay, Beth? God, you just looked so scared. It's amazing that some guys have absolutely no respect."

I nodded that I was okay and we just stood there holding onto one another, afraid to let go. A country song that David liked came one and we began slow-dancing. The male singer wanted to know who his girl was when he wasn't looking—like I needed a reason to feel lower than I already did, and David quietly sang the words along with him.

Later that night as we made love, he said, "You are mine—only mine." He repeated it several times throughout and I wasn't sure if he was trying to convince me or himself.

CHAPTER THIRTY-FOUR

I snap back to the present with that memory and find that I am still lying on the hardwood floor in the living room. It feels like I've been lying here for days.

Landon is sitting close to me, looking at something on his phone. He glances up at me, his face an unreadable mask, "You decide to join the land of the living again? I was just searching Google for tips on getting someone out of an anxiety-induced stupor." He laughs, but I can hear the worry behind his words.

I struggle to sit up and swallow, my mouth completely dry. When I speak, my voice sounds raspy due from all the crying, "It's true, then. All of it's true. You…and…me."

He puts his phone down and slides closer, sighing as he does so, "Yeah, it's true. It's a fucked up way to go about things, but it is what it is."

It's as if I'm drowning right now, emotions threatening to pull me under completely. Landon runs his thumbs across the back of my hand as I try to work out the tangled web of feelings running through me.

"Do you love me?" I blurt the words out before I've fully had a chance to think it through. Remembering his actions at the bar that night makes me regret asking almost immediately.

He doesn't even hesitate, "Yes, and you love me."

"But, David…" I trail off, realizing I don't even know how to finish the sentence.

Landon takes his free hand and massages his temples. "Fuck David. He's the reason you're in this mess in—" He stops talking and shifts gears almost seamlessly, "Have you slept with him?"

I don't even hesitate, "No, I just got out of the hospital. I'm still trying to sort out who I am." The lies slip so easily off my tongue and I feel like there's still something I'm missing here. *What am I still forgetting?*

He strokes my face, "Good girl," I've just managed to release the breath I've been holding when his hand slips down my face and rests it lightly against my throat, "You belong to—"

He's cut off by the sound of the garage opening and he and I both freeze in horror. He stands up, pulling me to him. There we stand, side by side, awaiting our fate.

David comes in and tosses his keys onto the island. "Beth? I decided they could manage on their own and drove like a mad-man to get—" The words die on his lips as he takes in the scene in front of him, "What the hell is going on here? Who the hell are you? Wait a minute—you're that fucker from the bar that night aren't you?"

I swallow the lump in my throat, "David, this is Landon," I pause and feel a bubble of hysterical laughter threatening me. *This cannot be real.* Landon glances over at me questioningly.

"Landon?" I see the exact moment the confusion on his face is replaced by knowledge, "Landon Scott. The man you thought you were married to. So how the fuck do you know my wife?"

Landon balls his hands into fists, the veins standing out on his forearms. He looks every bit the fighter ready to step into the ring. I place my hand on his arm and turn to my husband. "David, I'm sorry." My vision blurs with tears and I find that I can't say anything further.

"You've been sleeping with him?" He's running his hands through his hair and pacing. He looks like he wants to murder Landon. Or me. Perhaps both of us.

I open my mouth, my mind racing over what to say. Landon interjects before I come up with any sort of answer.

"What's it to you, David? Why is she all of a sudden so important to you?"

David stalks towards him, "Did I ask you, motherfucker? Do I look like I want to hear a fucking thing from you? She's my wife! I don't share!"

Landon takes a step towards him and I'm now caught in between them. Landon laughs sarcastically, "What are you gonna do, David? You think fighting me will make you a good husband?"

David raises his fist, "Let's find out—"

Landon doesn't flinch, "I know, David. I know what you're not man enough to tell her."

I gawk at Landon and back over at David. *What is he not man enough to tell me?* "David?"

He takes a step back and sits on the arm of the sofa. All the fight is gone from his eyes, replaced by resignation. "Beth…" He reaches for me and I take a step back, "I fucked up." I know this is the first time he's ever told me this, but it triggers a memory.

I open the door to find Nate standing on the doorstep. He looks around for David.

"David's at work, Nate. What can I do for you?"

"I'm sorry to drop by unannounced, but I thought he'd be here. I couldn't reach him on his cell and I really need someone to help me get through this."

I can tell that I am the last person he wants to see right now, but he's been drinking and his resolve is weakening. I grab him a beer from the fridge and carefully place it on a coaster in front of him, before sitting back in my armchair with mine.

"You can talk to me...I mean, that is, if you want to talk."

He tips the bottle back and downs almost half of it before responding to me. "I left Jess. She was having an affair," He glares at me, "Did you know?"

My mouth hangs open and I shake my head. "Having an affair?? She said you cheated on her!"

He shrugs and chugs more of his beer. "Yeah, that sounds like something she would do. I've been with her for eight years—eight years—and I can't tell you for how many of those years she was faithful," He points an accusing finger at me, "You. You're her best friend."

I nod, not entirely sure if he's making a statement or questioning me. He gets up and walks over to the fireplace, his hands holding the bricks for support. I silently will him to take deep breaths and to not break anything in his anger. "You know for someone who was so eager to start a family, she sure didn't waste any time fucking it up."

Okay, that came out of left field. I throw my hand up in a 'wait' gesture. "I—you—what? Hold on, you mean you and Jess were still...um, intimate, while she was cheating?"

"Yeah, twice a week. Nothing changed in that department. You can see how I'd be a little thrown to catch her cheating."

He stares at mine and David's wedding portrait hanging over the mantle. Fearing he's about to start smashing things, I walk over and place my hand on his. He immediately pulls me to him, crushing me against his chest.

"I've been so awful to you, Elizabeth. I really don't deserve your sympathy right now. I just didn't see this coming." He holds me tighter and I can tell he's crying. I find myself on the verge of joining him...

"But, she said she found text messages on your phone... some woman wanted to know if she was asleep so you could go to her!"

He laughs bitterly, "Those were the texts I found on her phone. She was sending that to him!"

I make my way back to the present and both men are staring at me. David looks like he's waiting for someone to put him out of his misery and Landon's jaw is set in such a line that I expect to hear his teeth shatter at any moment.

I spit the words out, "Jess. You're the reason Nate left. She was sleeping with you."

Landon steps closer to me, his arm around my shoulders. I shrug him off and step away. No way does he get to play the good guy in all of this.

David's eyes fill with tears, "Beth, I swear to God. It was a mistake. I didn't mean to hurt you!"

"I didn't mean to hurt you! I swear to God! Wake up, baby. Stay with me, please!"

My eyes widen in horror, for what feels like the billionth time tonight, "Y-y-you caused the car wreck! It was your fault!"

David has tears streaming down his face now and he tries to make his way over to me. I recoil in disgust and Landon holds his hand up, "Give her some space, man." His tone holds no trace of anger anymore.

I glare at Landon, "I can speak for myself."

We're sitting and enjoying dinner, but David's phone keeps ringing. I tease him, "Can't they give you even one night off?"

He laughs, "Beth, you know none of them know how to tie their shoes without me," he hands the waitress his credit card and stands up, "I'm gonna run to the bathroom."

I'm playing a game on my phone when he comes back to the table. His face is ashen. I stand up and grab onto him, "David? Are you okay? Is it your heart?" I have sudden flashbacks of his dad and I'm worried.

He shakes his head, "No, no nothing like that. I just got some bad news on a job. Let's get out of here."

He's silent as we make our way home. He picks up speed and begins weaving in and out of traffic. "David, slow down, please. What's the rush?"

He doesn't answer me. It's like he's in another world. The light ahead turns red, but he shows no signs of slowing down. We plow through the intersection and I'm able to scream out his name just as we collide with another vehicle. The teenage driver has a horrified look on his face. Glass is flying and my head hits the frame before everything goes dark.

I make my way over until I am standing in front of him. Landon moves behind me, and I find myself pissed off by his protectiveness, even in the midst of this shit storm.

"David, what happened the night of the accident?"

He places his head in his hands, refusing to make eye contact. His voice comes out as a whisper and I find myself leaning closer so that I can understand him.

"Jess kept calling. I called her back and she told me..." He pauses to compose himself, "She's pregnant, Beth. I fucked it all up."

Landon makes a sound and I turn to look at him, my expressions mirroring his. *He's just as thrown as I am.*

David latches onto my arms, pulling me into him. I struggle to break free, "Get your hands off of me. Get your goddamn hands off me!" I'm weeping, but the urge to hit him is strong. I howl with rage, "How could you do this? My best friend?" I raise my fist and Landon pulls me back.

"Beth, please let me fix this."

"How in the fuck are you going to fix this? You let her come to the hospital. I told her everything! If we were fighting, she knew. She used all of that information to drive a wedge between us. You two deserve each other!"

His head shoots up and he's on his feet in seconds, "Yeah, I messed up! I take full responsibility for that. Don't forget that you've been fucking this guy behind my back though. Your hands are just as dirty as mine!"

Landon's fist comes up and I step between him and David. "Landon, go. I need you to leave right now."

He shoots me an incredulous look, "You're kidding me right now! After that admission, you want *me* to leave?"

"I can't do this right now. I can't process all of this at once. Get. The. Fuck. Out!" My hands come up and maneuver him to the front door. If looks could kill, I'd be a pile of ashes right now.

His voice is cold, "You're going to regret this, Elizabeth." He turns away from me and storms out, slamming the door behind him.

I take one last look as his taillights illuminate the darkness, before turning back to David. He still sitting in the same position on the couch. As if sensing the mood change, the music shifts to something more somber. Birdy's voice is almost haunting as she sings about how she was the one worth leaving.

My head is pounding, from the accident and in an attempt to process the influx of memories. David's voice startles me, "Beth, I'm so sorry."

I stand frozen, my hand using the wall for support. "David, when did it start?" I must be a masochist to need these details.

He keeps his eyes downcast as his hand strokes his beard. "Right after my Dad died—and then the night you admitted you were on birth control. I took off and ended up drunk in a bar. She showed up and uh, one thing led to another."

There is nothing sweet about my tears. It's ugly. My nose is running and I'm making hiccupping sounds. David comes over and attempts to embrace me. "Please let me hold you, Beth." His voice is just above a whisper and a part of me wants nothing more than to cling to him until the hurt goes away.

"This is why I thought you both hated each other isn't it? Jesus, David." I gasp as another sob works its way out. *This has definitely turned into a nightmare.*

He takes another step toward me, "Beth, baby, I fucked up. I don't know what to do to fix this!"

I place my hands on his chest, pushing him away. "Get out. I can't—just leave."

My voice is so soft I'm not sure if he's even heard me until I see his hands come up to roughly rub at his eyes, "Please don't do this. Let's talk this out."

"I-I-I need y-you to leave, r-right now!" I try to sound authoritative, but with as hard as I'm crying, I sound more like I have a speech impediment.

He holds his hands up, "C'mon, baby, calm down. If you want me to leave, I'll leave. This isn't over though. You owe me just as many answers," he turns back to me before reaching the front door, "Dammit, Beth. You can't play the victim in this either. You fucked me over too!"

I scream and grab a figurine from the mantle before launching it at his head. It shatters when it hits the wall next to him. "Just leave!"

I sink down to the floor as he storms out, my crying has turned to wailing. My head feels as though it may explode. *Deep breaths. Don't panic. Everything is going to be okay.*

EPILOGUE

DAVID

I sit in my truck on the street outside the house. There's no way in hell I'm leaving her here alone. I can't believe it's turned into this. I knew my lies were a ticking time bomb, ready to explode at any minute, once Jess announced she was pregnant.

"Fuck!" I slam my hand into the steering wheel. *How did it come to this? When did we become not enough for each other?*

The situation is so beyond fucked up that I don't even know how to begin fixing it. I told Jess I wanted a paternity test the night she told me—it seems like so long ago. The night I almost lost my world.

I refuse to accept that Beth isn't mine anymore. She's been by my side for so long, I can't even begin to imagine her not there. *No, by God, I'm gonna fix this fucking mess.* There is only one woman I want in my bed the rest of my life and that's Beth. I can't believe it took almost losing her in a car accident to realize it. I'll either get her back or die trying. Landon Scott won't lay a hand on her as long as I'm around. If he tries, he's a dead man.

To be continued…

ABOUT THE AUTHOR

Shannon is a born and raised Texan. She grew up inventing clever stories, usually to get herself out of trouble. Her mother was not amused. In junior high, she began writing fractured fairy tales from the villain's point of view and that was the moment she knew that she was going to use her powers for evil instead of good.

In 2003, she moved to Denver and met the love of her life. After some relentless stalking and a few well-timed sarcastic remarks, the man eventually gave in to her charms and wifed her so hard. They welcomed a son in 2007 that they named after their favorite Marvel superhero, Spiderman.

Sick of seeing beautiful mountains through their window every day, the three escaped back to the desolate landscape of the west Texas desert in 2009. She welcomed her second son not long after and soon realized that being surrounded by three men was nothing at all like she'd imagined in her fantasies.

After an unplanned surgery in 2014 and a long pity party, she decided to pen a novel about the worst thing that could happen to a person in order to cheer herself up. She's twisted like that. Thus, From This Day Forward was born and the rest, as they say, is history.

Not only does Shannon enjoy stalking people, she also has a fondness for being stalked. Visit her at www.shannonshaemyers.com to keep up with her latest schemes and shenanigans.

ACKNOWLEDGMENTS

This book would not have been possible without the help of some amazing people.

I want to start by thanking my family for their patience while I was writing this. I really do have the best husband and kids around. They are always so supportive of me.

To Stephanie- you pushed me to give Beth a proper ending and I only hated you a little bit for it. You have been the best beta reader and I'm so happy I get to call you my friend.

To Rebecca Marie- Thank you for designing such a beautiful cover that really captures who these characters are to me, and for being so responsive to my five thousand emails explaining the subtleties of my fictional characters.

To my work girls- You know who you are. Thank you for pulling a broken person out of her shell and showing her what true friends are.